DATE DUE

JAN 1 4 2011			

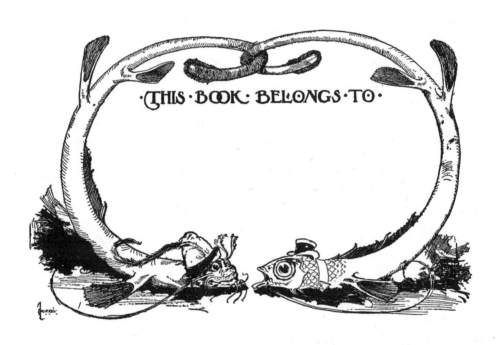

·THIS·BOOK·BELONGS·TO·

Classic Oz Tales
from
Books of Wonder®

The Sea Fairies
by L. Frank Baum
Illustrated by John R. Neill

Dot and Tot of Merryland
by L. Frank Baum
Newly Illustrated by
Donald Abbott

Captain Salt in Oz
by Ruth Plumly Thompson
Illustrated by John R. Neill

The Silver Princess in Oz
by Ruth Plumly Thompson
Illustrated by John R. Neill

The Wonder City of Oz
Written and Illustrated by
John R. Neill

Lucky Bucky in Oz
Written and Illustrated by
John R. Neill

The Magical Mimics in Oz
by Jack Snow
Illustrated by Frank Kramer

Sky Island
by L. Frank Baum
Illustrated by John R. Neill

Merry Go Round in Oz
by Eloise Jarvis McGraw
and Lauren McGraw
Illustrated by Dick Martin

Handy Mandy in Oz
by Ruth Plumly Thompson
Illustrated by John R. Neill

Ozoplaning with the Wizard
by Ruth Plumly Thompson
Illustrated by John R. Neill

The Scalawagons of Oz
Written and Illustrated by
John R. Neill

The Runaway in Oz
by John R. Neill
Illustrated by Eric Shanower

The Shaggy Man of Oz
by Jack Snow
Illustrated by Frank Kramer

If you enjoy the Oz books and want to know more about Oz, you may be interested in **The Royal Club of Oz**. Devoted to America's favorite fairyland, it is a club for everyone who loves the Oz books. For free information, please send a first-class stamp to:

The Royal Club of Oz
P.O. Box 714
New York, New York 10011

Or call toll-free: (800) 835-4315

Sea fairies

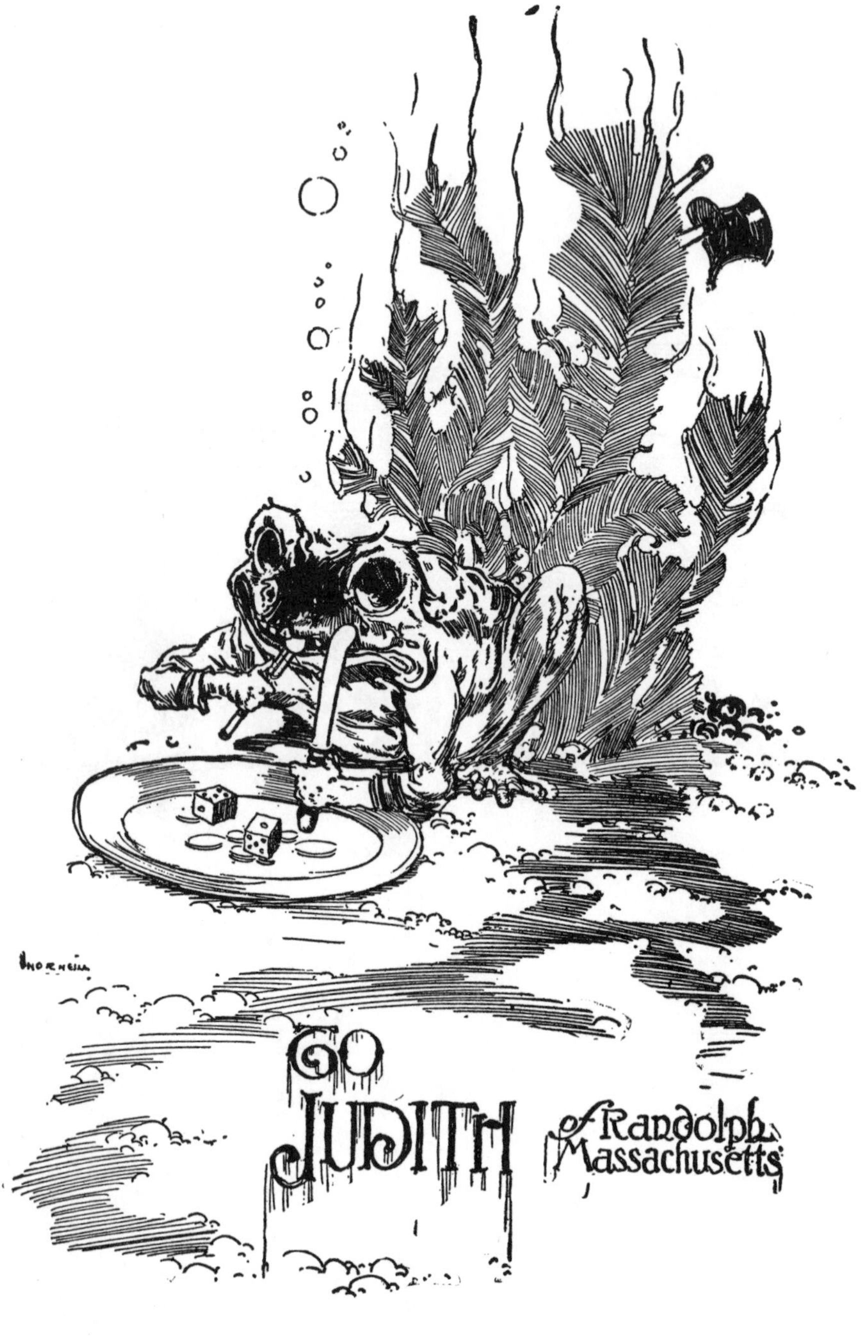
TO JUDITH
of Randolph Massachusetts

THE SEA FAIRIES

BY

L. FRANK BAUM

AUTHOR OF THE EMERALD CITY OF OZ, DOROTHY AND THE
WIZARD IN OZ, OZMA OF OZ, THE ROAD TO OZ,
THE LAND OF OZ, Etc.

ILLUSTRATED BY
JOHN R. NEILL

—

BOOKS OF WONDER

Cop. 1

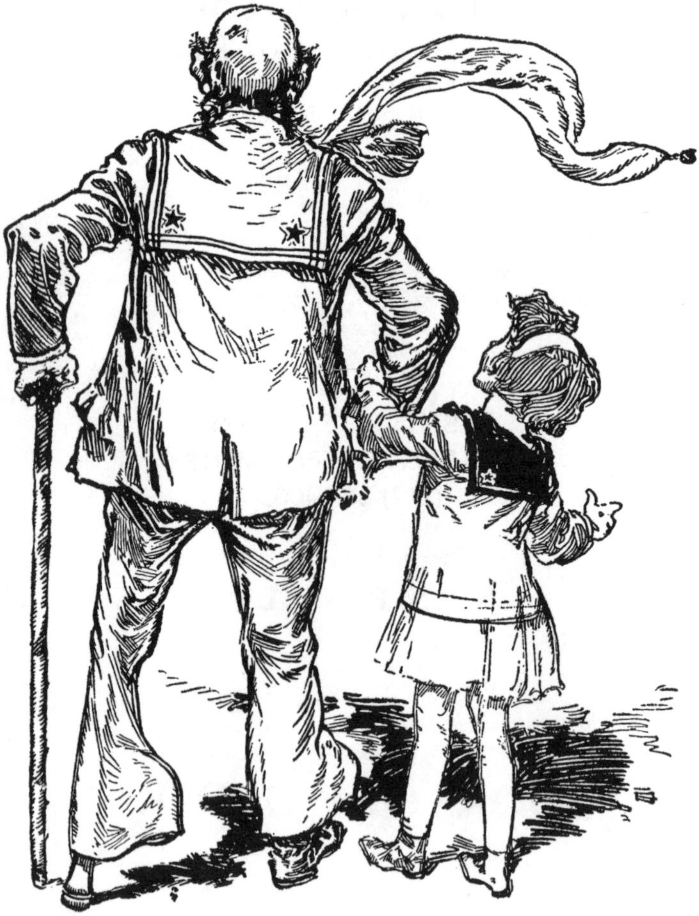

Books of Wonder,
132 Seventh Avenue,
New York, NY 10011.

4 5 6 7 8 9 10

THE oceans are big and broad. I believe two-thirds of the earth's surface is covered with water. What people inhabit this water has always been a subject of curiosity to the inhabitants of the land. Strange creatures come from the seas at times, and perhaps in the ocean depths are many, more strange than mortal eye has ever gazed upon.

This story is fanciful. In it the sea people talk and act much as we do, and the mermaids especially are not unlike the fairies with whom we have learned to be familiar. Yet they are real sea people, for all that, and with the exception of Zog the Magician they are all supposed to exist in the ocean's depths.

I am told that some very learned people deny that mermaids or sea-serpents have ever inhabited the oceans, but it would be very difficult for them to prove such an assertion unless they had lived under the water as Trot and Cap'n Bill did in this story.

I hope my readers who have so long followed Dorothy's adventures in the Land of Oz will be interested in Trot's equally strange experiences. The ocean has always appealed to me as a veritable wonderland, and this story has been suggested to me many times by my young correspondents in their letters. Indeed, a good many children have implored me to "write something about the mermaids," and I have willingly granted the request.

Hollywood, 1911.   L. FRANK BAUM.

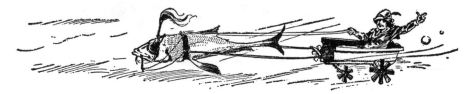

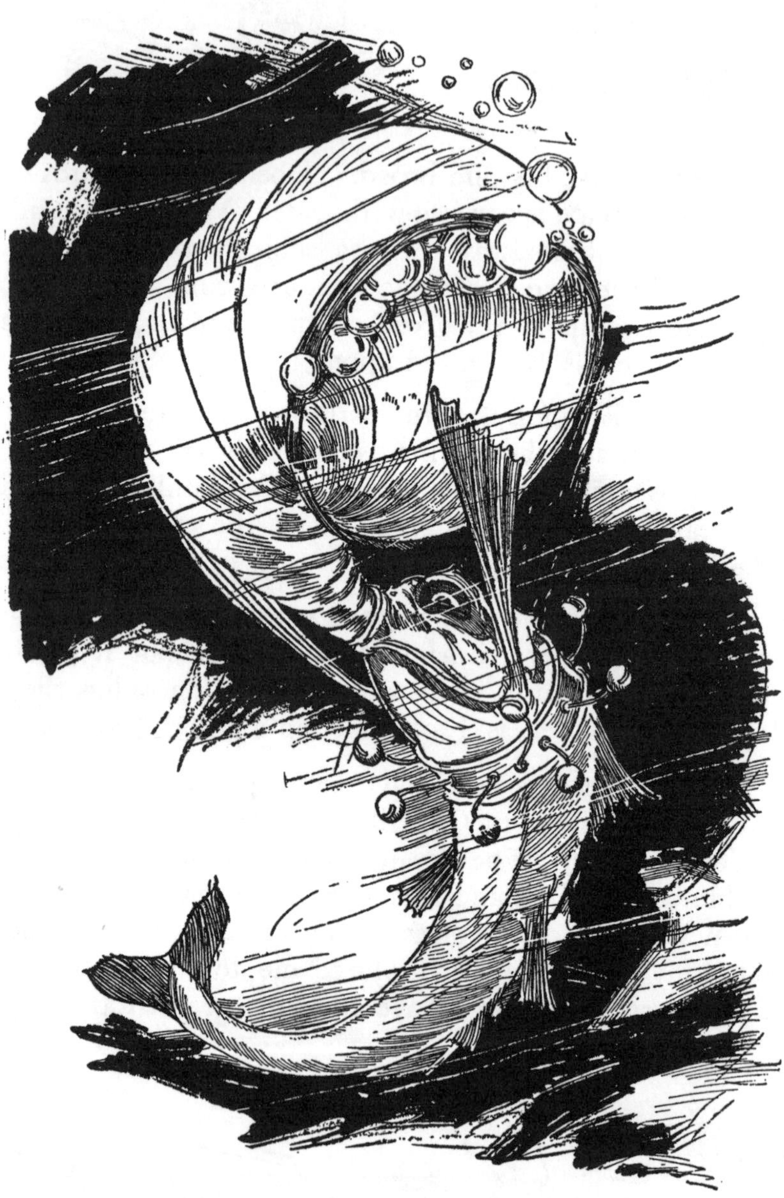

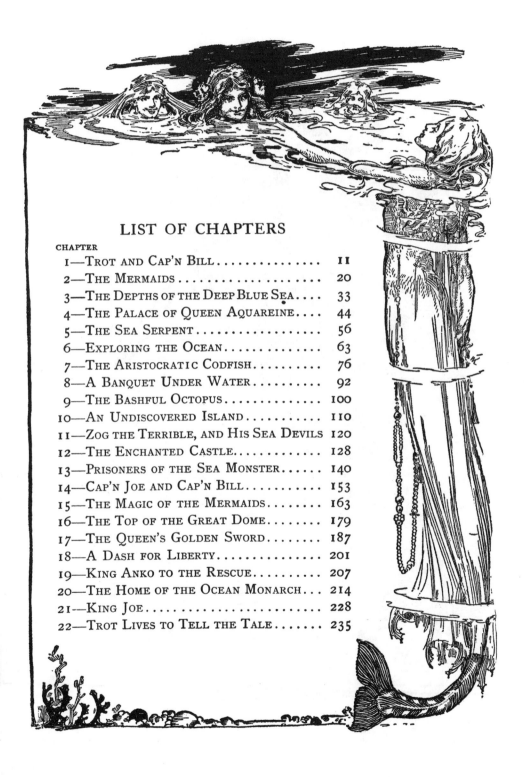

LIST OF CHAPTERS

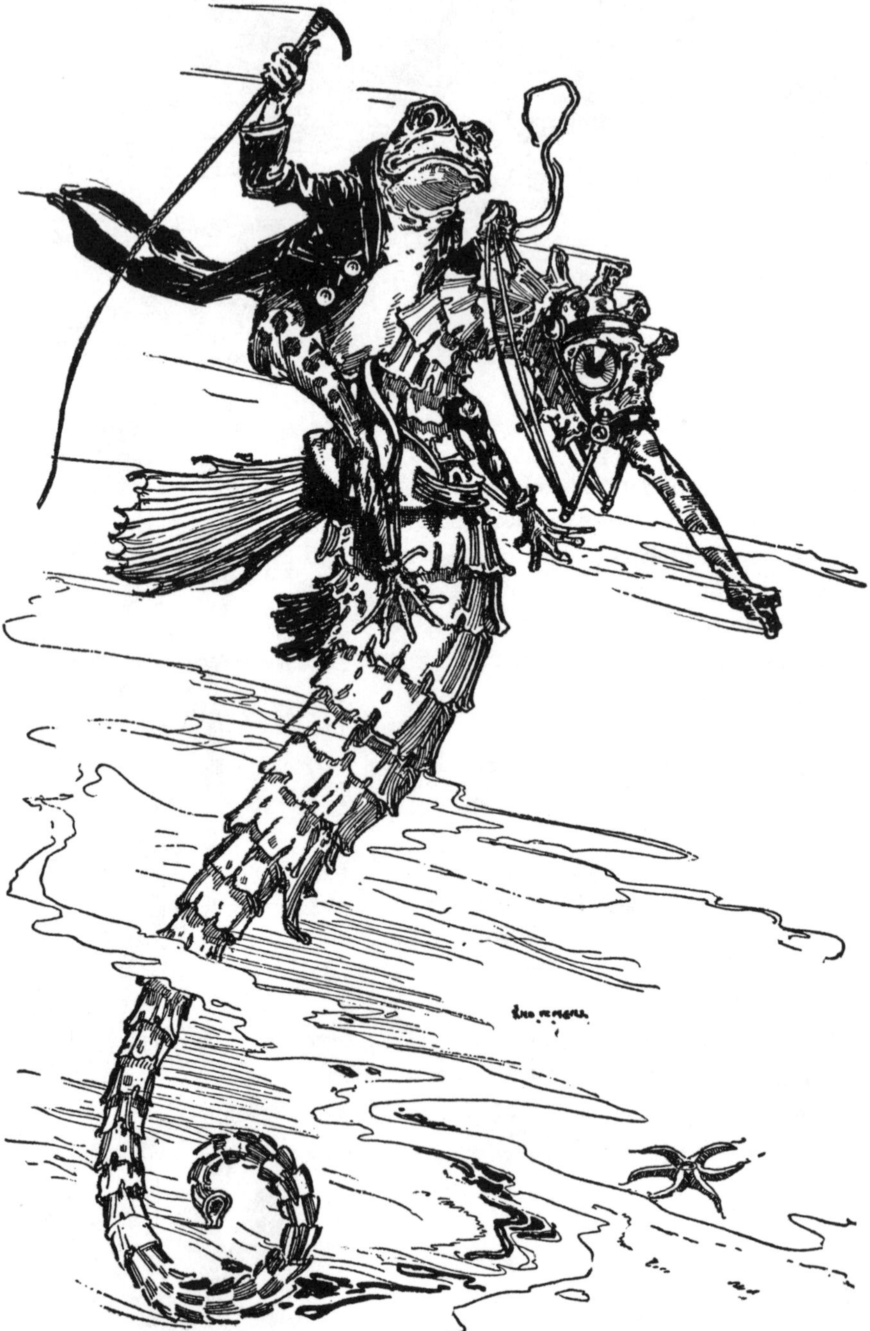

TROT AND CAP'N BILL Chap 1.

"NOBODY," said Cap'n Bill, solemnly, "ever sawr a mermaid an' lived to tell the tale."

"Why not?" asked Trot, looking earnestly up into the old sailor's face.

They were seated on a bench built around a giant acacia tree that grew just at the edge of the bluff. Below them rolled the blue waves of the great Pacific. A little way behind them was the house, a neat frame cottage painted white and surrounded by huge eucalyptus and pepper trees. Still farther behind that—a quarter of a mile distant but built upon a bend of the coast—was the village, overlooking a pretty bay.

Cap'n Bill and Trot came often to this tree, to sit and watch the ocean below them. The sailor man had one "meat leg" and one "hickory leg," and he often said the wooden

one was the best of the two. Once Cap'n Bill had commanded and owned the "Anemone," a trading schooner that
plied along the coast; and in those days Charlie Griffiths,
who was Trot's father, had been the Captain's mate. But
ever since Cap'n Bill's accident, when he lost his leg, Charlie
Griffiths had been the captain of the little schooner while his
old master lived peacefully ashore with the Griffiths family.

This was about the time Trot was born, and the old sailor
became very fond of the baby girl. Her real name was
Mayre, but when she grew big enough to walk she took so
many busy little steps every day that both her mother and
Cap'n Bill nicknamed her "Trot," and so she was thereafter
mostly called.

It was the old sailor who taught the child to love the
sea—to love it almost as much as he and her father did—and
these two, who represented the "beginning and the end of
life" became firm friends and constant companions.

"Why has n't anybody seen a mermaid and lived?"
asked Trot, again.

" 'Cause mermaids is fairies, an' ain't meant to be seen
by us mortal folk," replied Cap'n Bill.

"But if anyone happens to see 'em, what then, Cap'n?"

"Then," he answered, slowly wagging his head, "the
mermaids give 'em a smile an' a wink, an' they dives into the
water an' gets drownded."

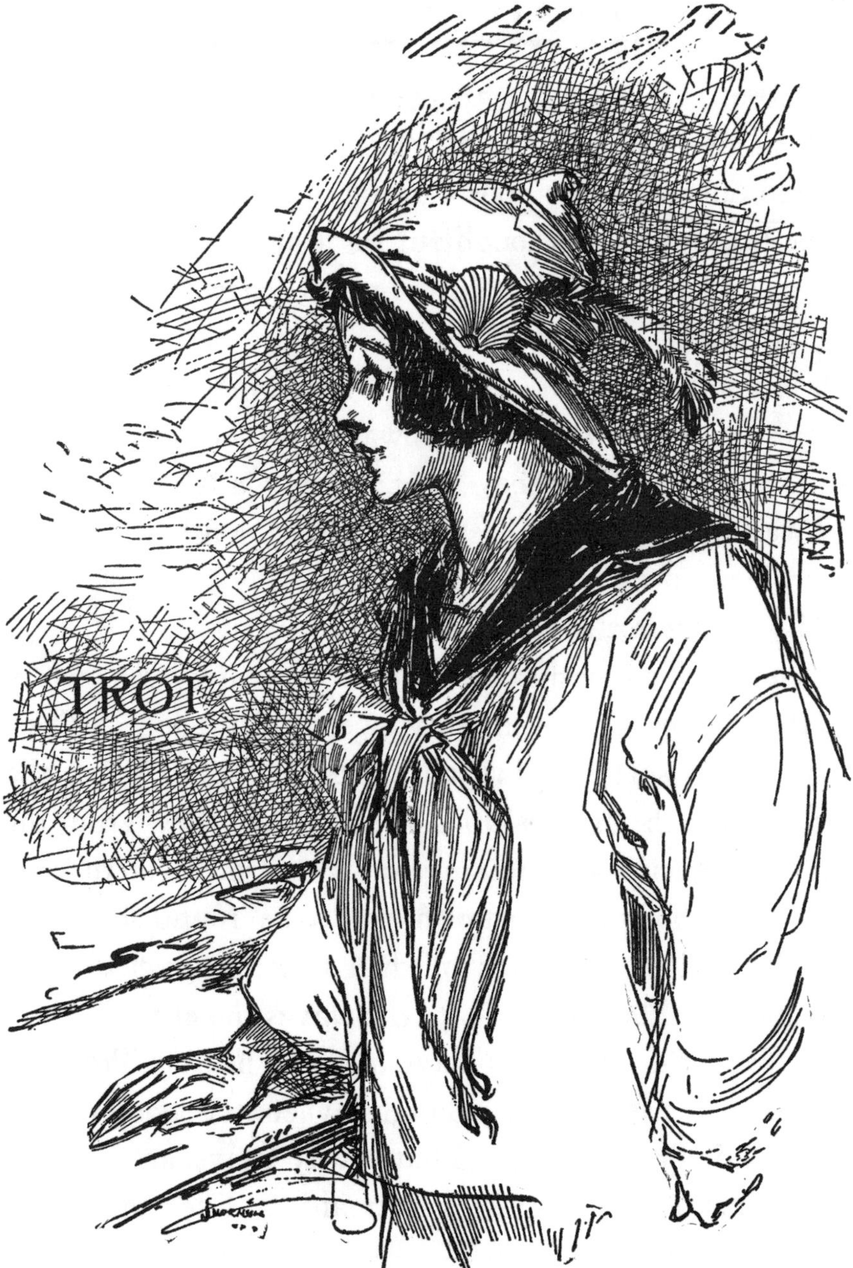
TROT

The Sea Fairies

"S'pose they know how to swim, Cap'n Bill?"

"That don't make any diff'rence, Trot. The mermaids live deep down, an' the poor mortals never come up again."

The little girl was thoughtful for a moment.

"But why do folks dive in the water when the mermaids smile an' wink?" she asked.

"Mermaids," he said, gravely, "is the most beautifulest creatures in the world—or the water, either. You know what they 're like, Trot; they 's got a lovely lady's form down to the waist, an' then the other half of 'em 's a fish, with green an' purple an' pink scales all adown it."

"Have they got arms, Cap'n Bill?"

"'Course, Trot; arms like any other lady. An' pretty faces that smile an' look mighty sweet an' fetchin'. Their hair is long an' soft an' silky, an' floats all around 'em in the water. When they comes up atop the waves they wring the water out 'n their hair and sing songs that go right to your heart. If anybody is unlucky enough to be 'round jes' then, the beauty o' them mermaids an' their sweet songs charm 'em like magic; so 's they plunge into the waves to get to the mermaids. But the mermaids have n't any hearts, Trot, no more 'n a fish has; so they laughs when the poor people drown, an' don't care a fig. That 's why I says, an' I says it true, that nobody never sawr a mermaid an' lived to tell the tale."

14

"Nobody?" asked Trot.

"Nobody a tall."

"Then how do you know, Cap'n Bill?" asked the little girl, looking up into his face with big round eyes.

Cap'n Bill coughed. Then he tried to sneeze, to gain time. Then he took out his red cotton handkerchief and wiped his bald head with it, rubbing hard so as to make him think clearer.

"Look, Trot; ain't that a brig out there?" he inquired, pointing to a sail far out in the sea.

"How does anybody know about mermaids, if those who have seen them never lived to tell about them?" she asked again.

"Know what about 'em, Trot?"

"About their green and pink scales, and pretty songs, and wet hair."

"They don't know, I guess. But mermaids jes' natcherly has to be like that, or they would n't be mermaids."

She thought this over.

"Somebody *must* have lived, Cap'n Bill," she declared, positively. "Other fairies have been seen by mortals; why not mermaids?"

"P'raps they have, Trot; p'raps they have," he answered, musingly. "I 'm tellin' you as it was told to me; but I never stopped to inquire into the matter so clost, before. Seems like folks would n't know so much about mermaids if they had n't seen 'em; an' yet accordin' to all accounts the victim is bound to get drownded."

"P'raps," suggested Trot, softly, "someone found a fotygraph of one of 'em."

"That might 'a' been, Trot; that might 'a' been," answered Cap'n Bill.

A nice man was Cap'n Bill, and Trot knew he always liked to explain everything so she could fully understand it. The aged sailor was not a very tall man, and some people might have called him chubby, or even fat. He wore a blue sailor shirt, with white anchors worked on the corners of the broad square collar, and his blue trousers were very wide at the bottom. He always wore one trouser leg over his wooden limb and sometimes it would flutter in the wind like a flag, because it was so wide and the wooden leg so slender. His rough kersey coat was a pea-jacket and came down to his waist line. In the big pockets of his jacket he kept a wonderful jackknife, and his pipe and tobacco, and many bits of string, and matches and keys and lots of other things. Whenever Cap'n Bill thrust a chubby hand into one of his pockets Trot watched him with breathless interest, for she never knew what he was going to pull out.

The old sailor's face was brown as a berry. He had a fringe of hair around the back of his head and a fringe of whisker around the edge of his face, running from ear to ear and underneath his chin. His eyes were light blue and kind in expression. His nose was big and broad and his few teeth were not strong enough to crack nuts with.

Trot liked Cap'n Bill and had a great deal of confidence

in his wisdom, and a great admiration for his ability to make tops and whistles and toys with that marvelous jackknife of his. In the village were many boys and girls of her own age, but she never had as much fun playing with them as she had wandering by the sea accompanied by the old sailor and listening to his fascinating stories.

The Sea Fairies

She knew all about the Flying Dutchman, and Davy Jones' Locker, and Captain Kidd, and how to harpoon a whale or dodge an iceberg, or lasso a seal. Cap'n Bill had been everywhere in the world, almost, on his many voyages. He had been wrecked on desert islands like Robinson Crusoe and been attacked by cannibals, and had a host of other exciting adventures. So he was a delightful comrade for the little girl, and whatever Cap'n Bill knew Trot was sure to know in time.

"How do the mermaids live?" she asked. "Are they in caves, or just in the water like fishes, or how?"

"Can't say, Trot," he replied. "I've asked divers about that, but none of 'em ever run acrost a mermaid's nest yet, as I've heard of."

"If they're fairies," she said, "their homes must be very pretty."

"Mebbe so, Trot; but damp. They're sure to be damp, you know."

"I'd like to see a mermaid, Cap'n Bill," said the child, earnestly.

"What, an' git drownded?" he exclaimed.

"No; and live to tell the tale. If they're beautiful, and laughing, and sweet, there can't be much harm in them, I'm sure."

"Mermaids is mermaids," remarked Cap'n Bill, in his

18

most solemn voice. "It would n't do us any good to mix up with 'em, Trot."

"May—re! May—re!" called a voice from the house.
"Yes, Mamma!"
"You an' Cap'n Bill come in to supper."

THE
MERMAIDS
Chap 2.

THE next morning, as soon as Trot had helped wipe tne breakfast dishes and put them away in the cupboard, the little girl and Cap'n Bill started out toward the bluff.

The air was soft and warm, and the sun turned the edges of the waves into sparkling diamonds. Across the bay the last of the fisherboats was speeding away out to sea, for well the fishermen knew this was an ideal day to catch rockbass, barracuda and yellowtail.

The old man and the young girl stood on the bluff and watched all this with interest. Here was their world.

"It is n't a bit rough this morning. Let 's have a boat ride, Cap'n Bill," said the child.

"Suits me to a T," declared the sailor.

So they found the winding path that led down the face of the cliff to the narrow beach below, and cautiously began

Chapter Two

the descent.   Trot never minded the steep path or the loose rocks at all; but Cap'n Bill's wooden leg was not so useful on a down grade as on a level, and he had to be careful not to slip and take a tumble.

But by and by they reached the sands and walked to a spot just beneath the big acacia tree that grew on the bluff. Halfway to the top of the cliff hung suspended a little shed like structure that sheltered Trot's rowboat, for it was necessary to pull the boat out of reach of the waves which beat in fury against the rocks at high tide.   About as high up as Cap'n Bill could reach was an iron ring, securely fastened to the cliff, and to this ring was tied a rope.   The old sailor unfastened the knot and began paying out the rope, and the rowboat came out of its shed and glided slowly downward to the beach.   It hung on a pair of davits, and was lowered just as a boat is lowered from a ship's side.   When it reached the sands the sailor unhooked the ropes and pushed the boat to the water's edge.   It was a pretty little craft, light and strong, and Cap'n Bill knew how to sail it or row it, as Trot might desire.

To-day they decided to row, so the girl climbed into the bow and her companion stuck his wooden leg into the water's edge, "so he would n't get his foot wet," and pushed off the little boat as he climbed aboard.   Then he seized the oars and began gently paddling.

21

"Whither away, Commodore Trot?" he asked gaily.

"I don't care, Cap'n. It's just fun enough to be on the water," she answered, trailing one hand overboard.

So he rowed around by the North Promontory, where the great caves were, and much as they were enjoying the ride they soon began to feel the heat of the sun.

"That's Dead Man's Cave, 'cause a skellington was found there," observed the child, as they passed a dark yawning mouth in the cliff. "And that's Bumble Cave, 'cause the bumblebees make nests in the top of it. And here's Smuggler's Cave, 'cause the smugglers used to hide things in it."

She knew all the caves well, and so did Cap'n Bill. Many of them opened just at the water's edge and it was possible to row their boat far into their dusky depths.

"And here's Echo Cave," she continued, dreamily, as they slowly moved along the coast; "and Giant's Cave, and —oh, Cap'n Bill! do you s'pose there were ever any giants in that cave?"

" 'Pears like there must 'a' been, Trot, or they would n't 'a' named it that name," he replied, pausing to wipe his bald head with the red handkerchief, while the oars dragged in the water.

"We 've never been into that cave, Cap'n," she remarked, looking at the small hole in the cliff—an archway through which the water flowed. "Let 's go in now."

"What for, Trot?"

"To see if there's a giant there."

"H-m. Aren't you 'fraid?"

"No; are you? I just don't b'lieve it's big enough for a giant to get into."

"Your father was in there once," remarked Cap'n Bill, "an' he says it's the biggest cave on the coast, but low down. It's full o' water, an' the water's deep down to the very bottom o' the ocean; but the rock roof's liable to bump your head at high tide."

"It's low tide now," returned Trot. "And how could any giant live in there if the roof is so low down?"

"Why, he couldn't, mate. I reckon they must have called it Giant's Cave 'cause it's so big, an' not 'cause any giant man lived there."

"Let's go in," said the girl, again; "I'd like to 'splore it."

"All right," replied the sailor. "It'll be cooler in there than out here in the sun. We won't go very far, for when the tide turns we mightn't get out again."

He picked up the oars and rowed slowly toward the cave. The black archway that marked its entrance seemed hardly big enough to admit the boat, at first; but as they drew nearer the opening became bigger. The sea was very calm here, for the headland shielded it from the breeze.

The Sea Fairies

"Look out fer your head, Trot!" cautioned Cap'n Bill, as the boat glided slowly into the rocky arch.

But it was the sailor who had to duck, instead of the little girl. Only for a moment, though. Just beyond the opening the cave was higher, and as the boat floated into the dim interior they found themselves on quite an extensive branch of the sea.

For a time neither of them spoke and only the soft lapping of the water against the sides of the boat was heard. A beautiful sight met the eyes of the two adventurers and held them dumb with wonder and delight.

It was not dark in this vast cave, yet the light seemed to come from underneath the water, which all around them glowed with an exquisite sapphire color. Where the little waves crept up to the sides of the rocks they shone like brilliant jewels, and every drop of spray seemed a gem fit to deck a queen.

Trot leaned her chin on her hands and her elbows on her lap and gazed at this charming sight with real enjoyment. Cap'n Bill drew in the oars and let the boat drift where it would, while he also sat silently admiring the scene.

Slowly the little craft crept farther and farther into the dim interior of the vast cavern, while its two passengers feasted their eyes on the beauties constantly revealed. Both the old seaman and the little girl loved the ocean in all its

24

Chapter Two

various moods. To them it was a constant companion and a genial comrade. If it stormed and raved they laughed with glee; if it rolled great breakers against the shore they clapped their hands joyfully; if it lay slumbering at their feet they petted and caressed it; but always they loved it.

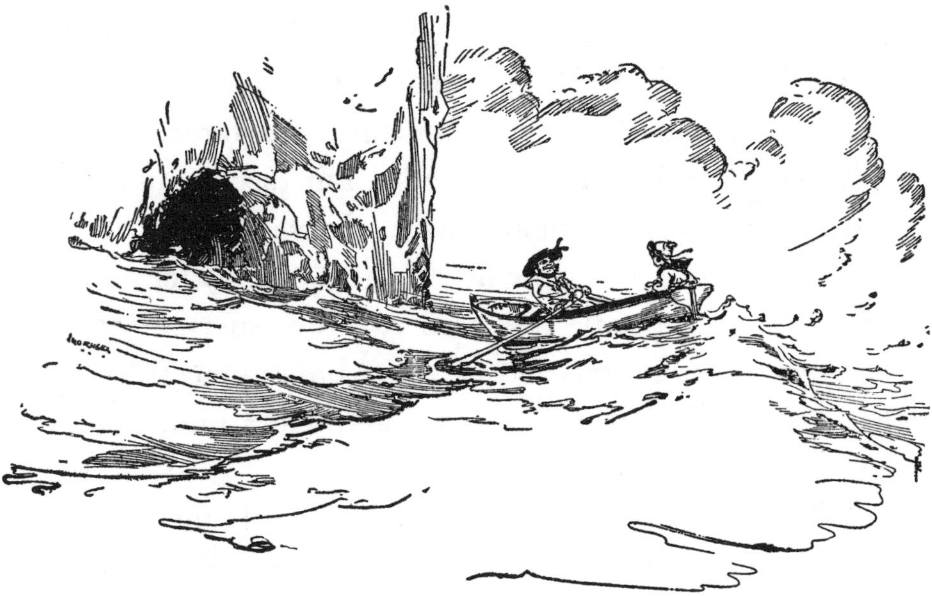

Here was the ocean yet. It had crept under the dome of overhanging rock to reveal itself crowned with sapphires and dressed in azure gown, revealing in this guise new and unsuspected charms.

"Good morning, Mayre," said a sweet voice.

Trot gave a start and looked around her in wonder. Just

The Sea Fairies

beside her in the water were little eddies—circles within circles—such as are caused when anything sinks below the surface.

"Did—did you hear that, Cap'n Bill?" she whispered, solemnly.

Cap'n Bill did not answer. He was staring, with eyes that fairly bulged out, at a place behind Trot's back, and he shook a little, as if trembling from cold.

Trot turned half around—and then she stared, too.

Rising from the blue water was a fair face around which floated a mass of long, blonde hair. It was a sweet, girlish face, with eyes of the same deep blue as the water and red lips whose dainty smile disclosed two rows of pearly teeth. The cheeks were plump and rosy, the brows gracefully penciled, while the chin was rounded and had a pretty dimple in it.

"The—the—most beauti-ful-est—in all the world!" murmured Cap'n Bill, in a voice of horror; "an' no one has ever lived to—to tell the tale!"

There was a peal of merry laughter, at this; laughter that rippled and echoed throughout the cavern. Just at Trot's side appeared a new face—even fairer than the other—with a wealth of brown hair wreathing the lovely features. And the eyes smiled kindly into those of the child.

"Are you—a—a—mermaid?" asked Trot, curiously.

26

Chapter Two

She was not a bit afraid. They seemed both gentle and friendly.

"Yes, dear," was the soft answer.

"We are all mermaids!" chimed a laughing chorus, and here and there, all about the boat, appeared pretty faces lying just upon the surface of the water.

"Are you part fishes?" asked Trot, greatly pleased by this wonderful sight.

"No, we are all mermaid," replied the one with the brown hair. "The fishes are partly like us, because they live in the sea and must move about. And you are partly like us, Mayre dear, but have awkward stiff legs so you may walk on the land. But the mermaids lived before fishes and before mankind, so both have borrowed something from us."

"Then you must be fairies, if you 've lived always," remarked Trot, nodding wisely.

"We are, dear; we are the water fairies," answered the one with the blonde hair, coming nearer and rising till her slender white throat showed plainly.

"We—we 're—goners, Trot!" sighed Cap'n Bill, with a white, woebegone face.

"I guess not, Cap'n," she answered calmly. "These pretty mermaids are n't going to hurt us, I 'm sure."

"No, indeed," said the first one who had spoken. "If we were wicked enough to wish to harm you our magic could reach you as easily upon the land as in this cave. But we love little girls dearly, and wish only to please them and make their lives more happy."

"I believe that!" cried Trot, earnestly.

Cap'n Bill groaned.

"Guess why we have appeared to you," said another mermaid, coming to the side of the boat.

"Why?" asked the child.

"We heard you say yesterday you would like to see a mermaid, and so we decided to grant your wish."

"That was real nice of you," said Trot, gratefully.

"Also we heard all the foolish things Cap'n Bill said about us," remarked the brown haired one, smilingly; "and we wanted to prove to him they were wrong."

"I on'y said what I've heard," protested Cap'n Bill. "Never havin' seen a mermaid afore, I could n't be ackerate; an' I never expected to see one an' live to tell the tale."

Again the cave rang with merry laughter, and as it died away Trot said:

"May I see your scales, please? And are they green and purple and pink, like Cap'n Bill said?"

They seemed undecided what to say to this, and swam a little way off, where the beautiful heads formed a group that was delightful to see. Perhaps they talked together, for the

"We-We're-Goners"

brown haired mermaid soon came back to the side of the boat and asked:

"Would you like to visit our kingdom, and see all the wonders that exist below the sea?"

"I'd like to," replied Trot, promptly; "but I could n't. I'd get drowned."

"That you would, mate!" cried Cap'n Bill.

"Oh, no," said the mermaid. "We would make you both like one of ourselves, and then you could live within the water as easily as we do."

"I don't know as I'd like it," said the child; "at least, for always."

"You need not stay with us a moment longer than you please," returned the mermaid, smiling as if amused at the remark. "Whenever you are ready to return home we promise to bring you to this place again and restore to you the same forms you are now wearing."

"Would I have a fish's tail?" asked Trot, earnestly.

"You would have a mermaid's tail," was the reply.

"What color would my scales be—pink, or purple?"

"You may choose the color yourself."

"Look a' here, Trot!" said Cap'n Bill, in excitement, "you ain't thinkin' o' doin' such a fool thing, are you?"

"'Course I am," declared the little girl. "We don't get

such inv'tations every day, Cap'n; and if I don't go now I may never find out how the mermaids live."

"I don't care how they live, myself," said Cap'n Bill. "I jes' want 'em to let *me* live."

"There 's no danger," insisted Trot.

"I do' know 'bout that. That 's what all the other folks said when they dove after the mermaids an' got drownded."

"Who?" asked the girl.

"I don't know who; but I 've heard tell—"

"You 've heard that no one ever saw a mermaid and lived," said Trot.

"To tell the tale," he added, nodding. "An' if we dives down, like they says, we won't live ourselves."

All the mermaids laughed at this, and the brown haired one said:

"Well, if you are afraid, don't come. You may row your boat out of this cave and never see us again, if you like. We merely thought it would please little Mayre, and were willing to show her the sights of our beautiful home."

"I 'd like to see 'em, all right," said Trot, her eyes glistening with pleasure.

"So would I," admitted Cap'n Bill; "if we would live to tell the tale."

"Don't you believe us?" asked the mermaid, fixing her

lovely eyes on those of the old sailor and smiling prettily. "Are you afraid to trust us to bring you safely back?"

"N—n—n-o," said Cap'n Bill; "'tain't that. I've got to look after Trot."

"Then you'll have to come with me," said Trot, decidedly, "for I'm going to 'cept this inv'tation. If you don't care to come, Cap'n Bill, you go home and tell mother I'm visitin' the mermaids."

"She'd scold me inter shivers!" moaned Cap'n Bill, with a shudder. "I guess I'd ruther take my chances down below."

"All right; I'm ready, Miss Mermaid," said Trot. "What shall I do? Jump in, clothes an' all?"

"Give me your hand, dear," answered the mermaid, lifting a lovely white arm from the water. Trot took the slender hand and found it warm and soft, and not a bit "fishy."

"My name is Clia," continued the mermaid, "and I am a princess in our deep-sea kingdom."

Just then Trot gave a flop and flopped right out of the boat into the water. Cap'n Bill caught a gleam of pink scales as his little friend went overboard, and the next moment there was Trot's face in the water, among those of the mermaids. She was laughing with glee as she looked up into Cap'n Bill's face and called:

"Come on in, Cap'n! It didn't hurt a bit!"

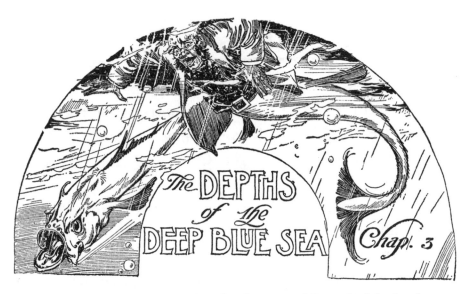

The DEPTHS of the DEEP BLUE SEA Chap. 3

CAP'N BILL stood up in the boat as if undecided what to do. Never a sailorman was more bewildered than this old fellow by the strangeness of the adventure he had encountered. At first he could hardly believe it was all true, and that he was not dreaming; but there was Trot in the water, laughing with the mermaids and floating comfortably about, and he could n't leave his dear little companion to make the trip to the depths of the ocean alone.

"Take my hand, please, Cap'n Bill," said Princess Clia, reaching her dainty arm toward him; and suddenly the old man took courage and clasped the soft fingers in his own. He had to lean over the boat to do this, and then there came a queer lightness to his legs and he had a great longing to be in the water. So he gave a flop and flopped in beside Trot, where he found himself comfortable enough, but somewhat frightened.

33

"Law sakes!" he gasped. "Here's me in the water with my rheumatics! I'll be that stiff termorrer I can't wiggle."

"You're wigglin' all right now," observed Trot. "That's a fine tail you've got, Cap'n, an' its green scales is jus' beautiful."

"Are they green, eh?" he asked, twisting around to try to see them.

"Green as em'ralds, Cap'n. How do they feel?"

"Feel, Trot—feel? Why, this tail beats that ol' wooden leg all holler! I kin do stunts now that I could n't 'a' done in a thousand years with ol' peg."

"And don't be afraid of the rheumatism," advised the Princess. "No mermaid ever catches cold or suffers pain in the water."

"Is Cap'n Bill a mermaid now?" asked Trot.

"Why, he's a mer*man*, I suppose," laughed the pretty princess. "But when he gets home he will be just Cap'n Bill again."

"Wooden leg an' all?" inquired the child.

"To be sure, my dear."

The sailor was now trying his newly-discovered powers of swimming, and became astonished at the feats he could accomplish. He could dart this way and that with wonderful speed, and turn and dive, and caper about in the water far better than he had ever been able to do on land—even before

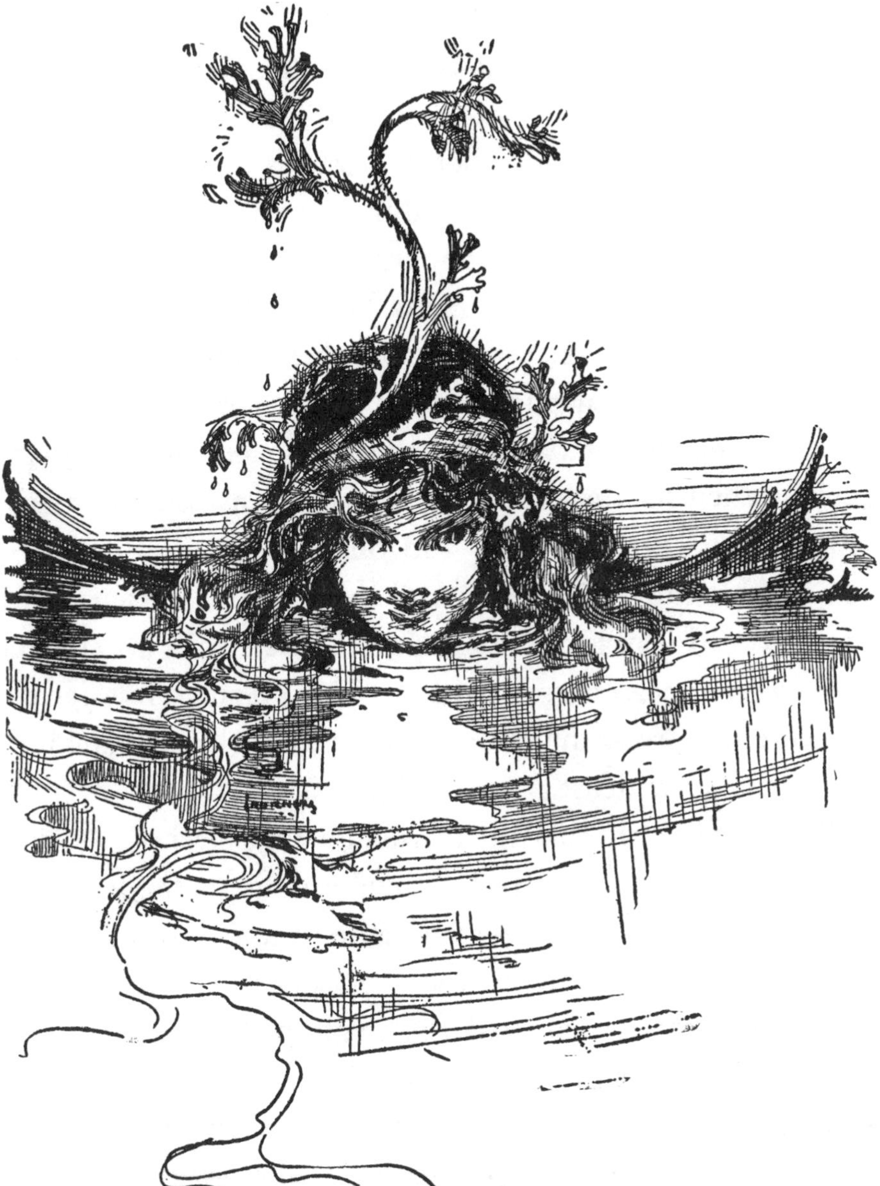

he got the wooden leg. And a curious thing about this present experience was that the water did not cling to him and wet him, as it had always done before. He still wore his flannel shirt and pea-jacket, and his sailor cap; but although he was in the water, and had been underneath the surface, the cloth still seemed dry and warm. As he dived down and came up again the drops flashed from his head and the fringe of beard, but he never needed to wipe his face or eyes at all.

Trot, too, was having queer experiences and enjoying them. When she ducked under water she saw plainly everything around her, as easily and distinctly as she had ever seen anything above water. And by looking over her shoulder she could watch the motion of her new tail, all covered with pretty iridescent pink scales, which gleamed like jewels. She wore her dress, the same as before, and the water failed to affect it in the least.

She now noticed that the mermaids were clothed, too, and their exquisite gowns were the loveliest things the little girl had ever beheld. They seemed made of a material that was like sheeny silk, cut low in the neck and with wide flowing sleeves that seldom covered the shapely white arms of her new friends. The gowns had trains that floated far behind the mermaids as they swam, but were so fleecy and transparent that the sparkle of their scales might be seen reaching back of their waists, where the human form ended and the fish part began. The sea fairies wore strings of splendid pearls twined around their throats, while more pearls were sewn upon their gowns for trimmings. They did not dress their beautiful hair at all, but let it float around them in clouds.

The little girl had scarcely time to observe all this when the princess said:

"Now, my dear, if you are ready we will begin our journey, for it is a long way to our palaces."

"All right," answered Trot, and took the hand extended to her with a trustful smile.

"Will you allow me to guide you, Cap'n Bill?" asked the blonde mermaid, extending her hand to the old sailor.

"O' course, ma'am," he said, taking her fingers rather bashfully.

"My name is Merla," she continued, "and I am cousin to Princess Clia. We must all keep together, you know, and I will hold your hand to prevent your missing the way."

While she spoke they began to descend through the water, and it grew quite dark for a time because the cave shut out the light. But presently Trot, who was eagerly looking around her, began to notice the water lighten and saw they were coming into brighter parts of the sea.

"We have left the cave now," said Clia, "and may swim straight home."

The Sea Fairies

"I s'pose there are no winding roads in the ocean," remarked the child, swimming swiftly beside her new friend.

"Oh, yes, indeed. At the bottom the way is far from being straight or level," replied Clia. "But we are in mid-water now, where nothing will hinder our journey, unless—"

She seemed to hesitate; so Trot asked: "Unless what?"

"Unless we meet with disagreeable creatures," said the Princess. "The mid-water is not as safe as the very bottom, and that is the reason we are holding your hands."

"What good would that do?" asked Trot.

"You must remember that we are fairies," said Princess Clia. "For that reason nothing in the ocean can injure us; but you two are mortals, and therefore not entirely safe at all times unless we protect you."

Trot was thoughtful for a few moments and looked around her a little anxiously. Now and then a dark form would shoot across their pathway, or pass them at some distance; but none was near enough for the girl to see plainly what it might be.

Suddenly they swam right into a big school of fishes, all yellowtails and of very large size. There must have been hundreds of them lying lazily in the water, and when they saw the mermaids they merely wiggled to one side and opened a path for the sea fairies to pass through.

"Will they hurt us?" asked Trot.

38

Chapter Three

"No, indeed," laughed the Princess. "Fishes are stupid creatures mostly, and this family is quite harmless."

"How about sharks?" asked Cap'n Bill, who was swimming gracefully beside them, his hand clutched in that of pretty Merla.

"Sharks may indeed be dangerous to you," replied Clia; "so I advise you to keep them at a safe distance. They never dare attempt to bite a mermaid, and it may be they will think you belong to our band; but it is well to avoid them, if possible."

"Don't get careless, Cap'n," added Trot.

"I surely won't, mate," he replied. "You see, I did n't use to be 'fraid o' sharks, 'cause if they came near I 'd stick my wooden leg at 'em. But now, if they happens to fancy these green scales, it 's all up with ol' Bill."

"Never fear," said Merla; "I 'll take care of you on our journey, and in our palaces you will find no sharks at all."

"Can't they get in?" he asked, anxiously.

"No. The palaces of the mermaids are inhabited only by themselves."

"Is there anything else to be afraid of in the sea?" asked the little girl, after they had swum quite a while in silence.

"One or two things, my dear," answered Princess Clia. "Of course, we mermaids have great powers, being fairies;

yet among the sea people is one nearly as powerful as we are, and that is the devilfish."

"I know," said Trot; "I've seen 'em."

"You have seen the smaller ones, I suppose, which sometimes rise to the surface or go near shore, and are often caught by fishermen," said Clia; "but they are only second cousins of the terrible deep-sea devilfish to which I refer."

"Those ones are bad enough, though," declared Cap'n Bill. "If you know any worse ones I don't want a interduction to 'em."

"The monster devilfish inhabit caves in the rugged, mountainous regions of the ocean," resumed the Princess, "and they are evil spirits who delight in injuring all who meet them. None lives near our palaces, so there is little danger of your meeting any while you are our guests."

"I hope we won't," said Trot.

"None for me," added Cap'n Bill. "Devils of any sort ought to be give a wide berth, an' devilfishes is worser ner sea serpents."

"Oh, do you know the sea serpents?" asked Merla, as if surprised.

"Not much I don't," answered the sailor; "but I've heard tell of folks as has seen 'em."

"Did they ever live to tell the tale?" asked Trot.

"Sometimes," he replied. "They're jes' *or*-ful creatures, mate."

"How easy it is to be mistaken," said Princess Clia, softly. "We know the sea serpents very well, and we like them."

"You do!" exclaimed Trot.

"Yes, dear. There are only three of them in all the world, and not only are they harmless, but quite bashful and shy. They are kind-hearted, too, and although not beautiful in appearance, they do many kind deeds and are generally beloved."

"Where do they live?" asked the child.

"The oldest one, who is king of this ocean, lives quite near us," said Clia. "His name is Anko."

"How old is he?" inquired Cap'n Bill, curiously.

"No one knows. He was here before the ocean came, and he stayed here because he learned to like the water better than the land as a habitation. Perhaps King Anko is ten thousand years old—perhaps twenty thousand. We often lose track of the centuries down here in the sea."

"That's pretty old, isn't it," said Trot. "Older than Cap'n Bill, I guess."

"Summat," chuckled the sailorman; "summat older, mate; but not much. P'raps the sea serpent ain't got gray whiskers."

"Oh yes, he has," responded Merla, with a laugh. "And

41

so have his two brothers—Unko and Inko. They each have an ocean of their own, you know; and once every hundred years they come here to visit their brother Anko. So we've seen all three many times."

"Why, how old are mermaids, then?" asked Trot, looking around at the beautiful creatures wonderingly.

"We are like all ladies of uncertain age," rejoined the Princess, with a smile. "We don't care to tell."

"Older than Cap'n Bill?"

"Yes, dear," said Clia.

"But we haven't any gray whiskers," added Merla, merrily, "and our hearts are ever young."

Trot was thoughtful. It made her feel solemn to be in the company of such old people. The band of mermaids seemed, to all appearances, young and fresh and not a bit as if they'd been soaked in water for hundreds of years. The girl began to take more notice of the sea maidens following after her. More than a dozen were in the group; all very lovely in appearance and clothed in the same gauzy robes as Merla and the princess. These attendants did not join in the conversation, but darted here and there in sportive play, and often Trot heard the tinkling chorus of their laughter. Whatever doubts might have arisen in the child's mind, through the ignorant tales of her sailor friend, she now found the mermaids to be light-hearted, joyous and gay, and from the first she had not been in the least afraid of her new companions.

"How much farther do we have to go?" asked Cap'n Bill, presently.

"Are you getting tired?" Merla inquired.

"No," said he; "but I'm sorter anxious to see what your palaces look like. Inside the water ain't as interestin' as the top of it. It's fine swimmin', I'll agree; an' I like it; but there ain't nuthin' special to see, that I can make out."

"That is true, sir," replied the Princess. "We have purposely led you through the mid-water, hoping you would see nothing to alarm you until you get more accustomed to our ocean life. Moreover, we are able to travel more swiftly here. How far do you think we have already come, Cap'n?"

"Oh, 'bout two mile," he answered.

"Well, we are now hundreds of miles from the cave where we started," she told him.

"You don't mean it!" he exclaimed, in wonder.

"Then there's magic in it," announced Trot, soberly.

"True, my dear. To avoid tiring you, and to save time, we have used a little of our fairy power," said Clia. "The result is that we are nearing our home. Let us go downward a bit, now, for you must know that the mermaid palaces are at the very bottom of the ocean—and in its deepest part."

The
PALACE OF
QUEEN AQUARINE
Chap. 4

TROT was surprised to find it was not at all dark or gloomy
as they descended farther into the deep sea. Things were
not quite so clear to her eyes as they had been in the bright
sunshine above the ocean's surface, but every object was distinct, nevertheless, as if she saw it through a pane of green
tinted glass. The water was very clear, except for this green
shading, and the little girl had never before felt so light and
buoyant as she did now. It was no effort at all to dart through
the water, which seemed to support her on all sides.

"I don't believe I weigh anything at all," she told
Cap'n Bill.

"No more do I, Trot," said he. "But that's nat'ral, seein'
as we're under water so far. What bothers me most is how
we manage to breathe, havin' no gills, like fishes have."

44

"Are you sure we have n't any gills?" she asked, lifting her free hand to feel her throat.

"Sure. Ner the mermaids have n't any, either," declared Cap'n Bill.

"Then," said Trot, "we 're breathing by magic."

The mermaids laughed at this shrewd remark, and the Princess said:

"You have guessed correctly, my dear. Go a little slower, now, for the palaces are in sight."

"Where?" asked Trot, eagerly.

"Just before you."

"In that grove of trees?" inquired the girl. And, really, it seemed to her they were approaching a beautiful grove.

The bottom of the sea was covered with white sand, in which grew many varieties of sea shrubs with branches like those of trees. Not all of them were green, however, for the branches and leaves were of a variety of gorgeous colors. Some were purple, shading down to light lavender; and there were reds all the way from a delicate rose-pink to vivid shades of scarlet. Orange, yellow and blue shades were there, too, mingling with the sea-greens in a most charming manner. Altogether, Trot found the brilliant coloring somewhat bewildering.

These sea shrubs, which in size were quite as big and tall as the trees on earth, were set so close together that their branches entwined; but there were several avenues leading into the groves, and at the entrance to each avenue the girl noticed several large fishes, with long spikes growing upon their noses.

"These are swordfishes," remarked the Princess, as she led the band past one of these avenues.

"Are they dang'rous?" asked Trot.

"Not to us," was the reply. "The swordfishes are among our most valued and faithful servants, guarding the entrances to the gardens which surround our palaces. If any creatures try to enter uninvited these guards fight them and drive them away. Their swords are sharp and strong, and they are fierce fighters, I assure you."

"I 've known 'em to attack ships, an' stick their swords right through the wood," said Cap'n Bill.

"Those belonged to the wandering tribes of swordfishes," explained the Princess. "These, who are our servants, are too sensible and intelligent to attack ships."

The band now headed into a broad passage through the "gardens," as the mermaids called these gorgeous groves, and the great swordfishes guarding the entrance made way for them to pass, afterward resuming their posts with round and watchful eyes. As they slowly swam along the avenue Trot noticed that some of the bushes seemed to have fruits grow-

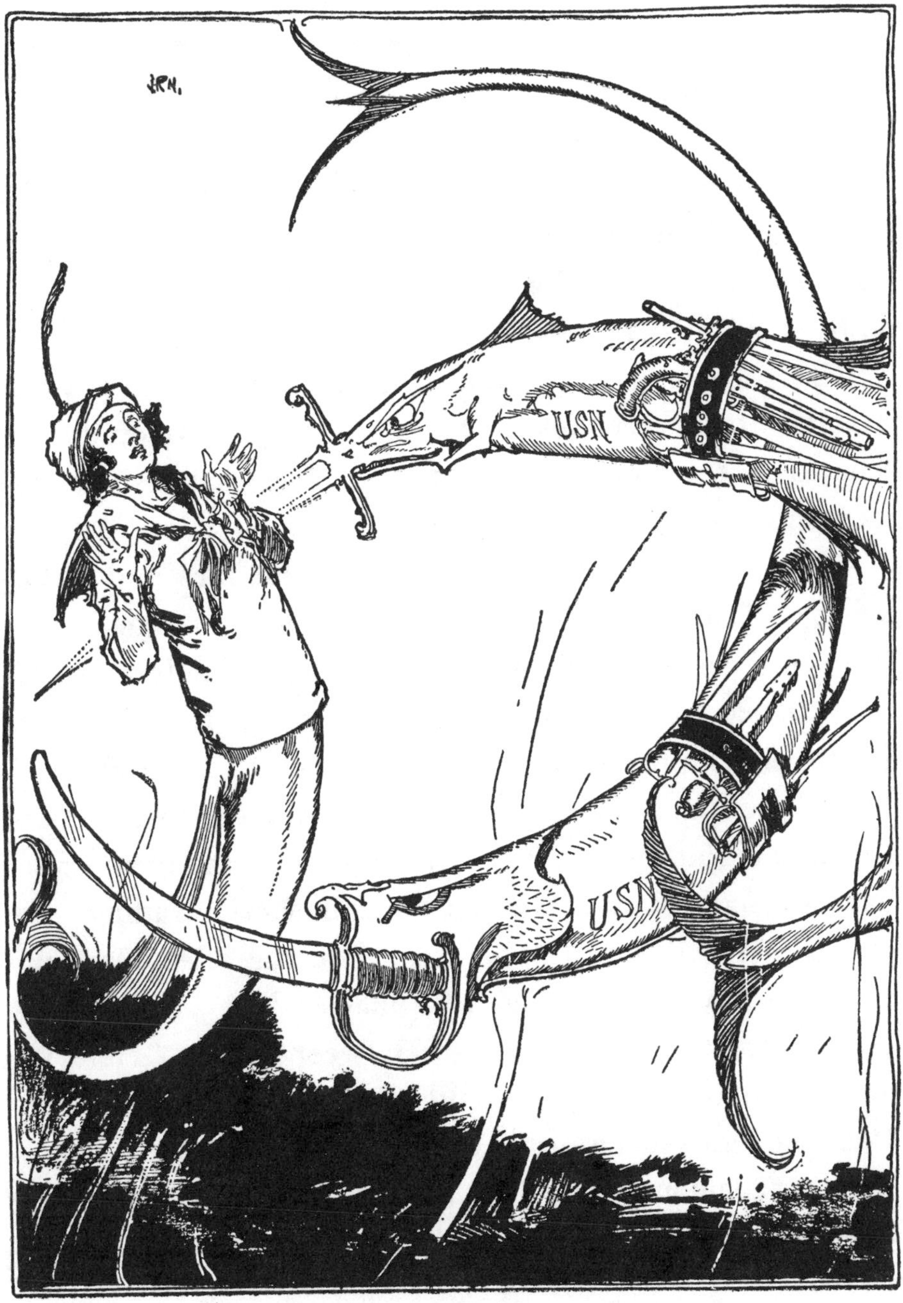
USN
USN

ing upon them; but what these fruits might be, neither she nor Cap'n Bill could guess.

The way wound here and there for some distance, till finally they came to a more open space, all carpeted with sea flowers of exquisite colorings. Although Trot did not know it, these flowers resembled the rare orchids of earth in their fanciful shapes and marvelous hues. The child did not examine them very closely, for across the carpet of flowers loomed the magnificent and extensive palaces of the mermaids.

These palaces were built of coral; white, pink and yellow being used, and the colors arranged in graceful designs. The front of the main palace, which now faced them, had circular ends connecting the straight wall, not unlike the architecture we are all familiar with; yet there seemed to be no windows to the building, although a series of archways served as doors.

Arriving at one of the central archways the band of sea maidens separated, Princess Clia and Merla leading Trot and Cap'n Bill into the palace, while the other mermaids swam swiftly away to their own quarters.

"Welcome!" said Clia, in her sweet voice. "Here you are surrounded only by friends and are in perfect safety. Please accept our hospitality as freely as you desire, for we consider you honored guests. I hope you will like our home," she added, a little shyly.

"We are sure to, dear Princess," Trot hastened to say.

Then Clia escorted them through the archway and into a lofty hall. It was not a mere grotto, but had smoothly built walls of pink coral inlaid with white. Trot at first thought there was no roof, for looking upward she could see the water all above them. But the princess, reading her thought, said with a smile:

"Yes, there is a roof, or we would be unable to keep all the sea people out of our palace. But the roof is made of glass, to admit the light."

"Glass!" cried the astonished child. "Then it must be an awful big pane of glass."

"It is," agreed Clia. "Our roofs are considered quite wonderful, and we owe them to the fairy powers of our queen. Of course, you understand there is no natural way to make glass under water."

"No, indeed," said Cap'n Bill. And then he asked: "Does your queen live here?"

"Yes. She is waiting now, in her throne room, to welcome you. Shall we go in?"

"I'd just as soon," replied Trot, rather timidly; but she boldly followed the princess, who glided through another arch into a small room, where several mermaids were reclining upon couches of coral. They were beautifully dressed and wore many sparkling jewels.

The Sea Fairies

"Her Majesty is awaiting the strangers, Princess Clia," announced one of these. "You are asked to enter at once."

"Come, then," said Clia, and once more taking Trot's hand she led the girl through still another arch, while Merla followed just behind them, escorting Cap'n Bill.

They now entered an apartment so gorgeous that the child fairly gasped with astonishment. The queen's throne room was indeed the grandest and most beautiful chamber in all the ocean palaces. Its coral walls were thickly inlaid with mother-of-pearl, exquisitely shaded and made into borders and floral decorations. In the corners were cabinets, upon the shelves of which many curious shells were arranged, all beautifully polished. The floor glittered with gems arranged in patterns of flowers, like a brilliant carpet.

Near the center of the room was a raised platform of mother-of-pearl upon which stood a couch thickly studded with diamonds, rubies, emeralds and pearls. Here reclined Queen Aquareine, a being so lovely that Trot gazed upon her spellbound and Cap'n Bill took off his sailor cap and held it in his hands.

All about the room were grouped other mother-of-pearl couches, not raised like that of the queen, and upon each of these reclined a pretty mermaid. They could not sit down as we do, Trot readily understood, because of their tails; but they rested very gracefully upon the couches, with their trailing gauzy robes arranged in fleecy folds.

When Clia and Merla escorted the strangers down the length of the great room toward the royal throne they met with pleasant looks and smiles on every side, for the sea maidens were too polite to indulge in curious stares. They paused just before the throne, and the queen raised her head upon one elbow to observe them.

"Welcome, Mayre," she said; "and welcome, Cap'n Bill. I trust you are pleased with your glimpse of the life beneath the surface of the sea."

"*I* am," answered Trot, looking admiringly at the beautiful face of the queen.

"It's all mighty cur'ous an' strange like," said the sailor, slowly. "I'd no idee you mermaids were like this, at all!"

"Allow me to explain that it was to correct your wrong ideas about us that led me to invite you to visit us," replied the Queen. "We usually pay little heed to the earth people, for we are content in our own dominions; but, of course, we know all that goes on upon your earth. So, when Princess Clia chanced to overhear your absurd statements concerning us, we were greatly amused and decided to let you see, with your own eyes, just what we are like."

"I'm glad you did," answered Cap'n Bill, dropping his

eyes in some confusion as he remembered his former description of the mermaids.

"Now that you are here," continued the Queen, in a cordial, friendly tone, "you may as well remain with us a few days and see the wonderful sights of our ocean."

"I'm much obliged to you, ma'am," said Trot; "and I'd like to stay, ever so much; but mother worries jus' dreadful if we don't get home in time."

"I'll arrange all that," said Aquareine, with a smile.

"How?" asked the girl.

"I will make your mother forget the passage of time, so she will not realize how long you are away. Then she cannot worry."

"Can you do that?" inquired Trot.

"Very easily. I will send your mother into a deep sleep that will last until you are ready to return home. Just at present she is seated in her chair by the front window, engaged in knitting." The queen paused to raise an arm and wave it slowly to and fro. Then she added: "Now your good mother is asleep, little Mayre, and instead of worries I promise her pleasant dreams."

"Won't somebody rob the house while she's asleep?" asked the child anxiously.

"No, dear. My charm will protect the house from any intrusion."

"That's fine!" exclaimed Trot in delight.

"It's jes' won-erful!" said Cap'n Bill. "I wish I knew it was so. Trot's mother has a awful sharp tongue when she's worrited."

"You may see for yourselves," declared the Queen, and waved her hand again.

At once they saw before them the room in the cottage, with Mayre's mother asleep by the window. Her knitting was in her lap and the cat lay curled up beside her chair. It was all so natural that Trot thought she could hear the clock over the fireplace tick. After a moment the scene faded away, when the queen asked with another smile: "Are you satisfied?"

"Oh, yes!" cried Trot. "But how could you do it?"

"It is a form of mirage," was the reply. "We are able to bring any earth scene before us whenever we wish. Sometimes these scenes are reflected above the water, so that mortals also observe them."

"I've seen 'em," said Cap'n Bill, nodding. "I've seen mirages; but I never knowed what caused 'em, afore now."

"Whenever you see anything you do not understand, and wish to ask questions, I will be very glad to answer them," said the Queen.

"One thing that bothers me," said Trot, "is why we don't get wet, being in the ocean with water all around us."

The Sea Fairies

"That is because no water really touches you," explained the Queen. "Your bodies have been made just like those of the mermaids, in order that you may fully enjoy your visit to us. One of our peculiar qualities is that water is never permitted to quite touch our bodies, or our gowns. Always there remains a very small space, hardly a hair's breadth

between us and the water, which is the reason we are always warm and dry."

"I see," said Trot. "That's why you don't get soggy, or withered."

"Exactly," laughed the Queen, and the other mermaids joined in her merriment.

Chapter Four

"I s'pose that 's how we can breathe without gills," remarked Cap'n Bill, thoughtfully.

"Yes; the air space is constantly replenished from the water, which contains air, and this enables us to breathe as freely as you do upon the earth."

"But we have fins," said Trot, looking at the fin that stood upright on Cap'n Bill's back.

"Yes; they allow us to guide ourselves as we swim, and so are very useful," replied the Queen.

"They make us more finished," said Cap'n Bill, with a chuckle. Then, suddenly becoming grave, he asked: "How 'bout my rheumatics, ma'am? Ain't I likely to get stiffened up with all this dampness?"

"No, indeed," Aquareine answered; "there is no such thing as rheumatism in all our dominions. I promise no evil result shall follow this visit to us, so please be as happy and contented as possible."

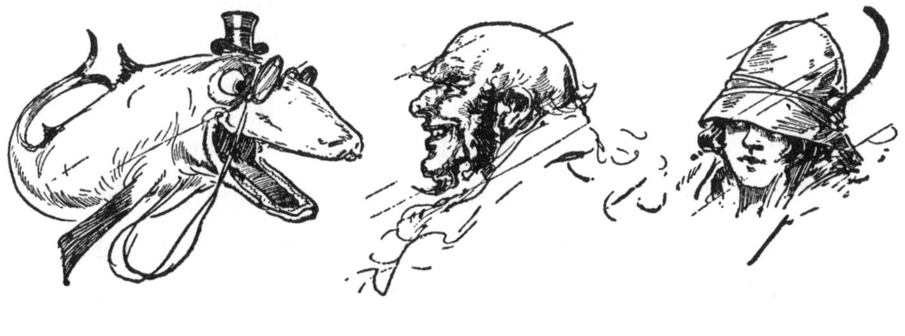

THE SEA-SERPENT

Chap 5.

JUST then Trot happened to look up at the glass roof and saw a startling sight. A big head, with a face surrounded by stubby gray whiskers, was poised just over them, and the head was connected with a long, curved body that looked much like a sewer pipe.

"Oh, there is King Anko," said the Queen, following the child's gaze. "Open a door and let him in, Clia, for I suppose our old friend is anxious to see the earth people."

"Won't he hurt us?" asked the little girl, with a shiver of fear.

"Who, Anko? Oh, no, my dear! We are very fond of the sea serpent, who is king of this ocean, although he does not rule the mermaids. Old Anko is a very agreeable fellow, as you will soon discover."

"Can he talk?" asked Trot.

"Yes, indeed."

"And can we understand what he says?"

"Perfectly," replied the Queen. "I have given you power, while you remain here, to understand the language of every inhabitant of the sea."

"That's nice," said Trot, gratefully.

The Princess Clia swam slowly to one of the walls of the throne room where, at a wave of her hand, a round hole appeared in the coral. The sea serpent at once observed this opening and the head left the roof of glass only to reappear presently at the round hole. Through this he slowly crawled, until his head was just beneath the throne of Queen Aquareine, who said to him:

"Good morning, your Majesty. I hope you are quite well?"

"Quite well, thank your Majesty," answered Anko; and then he turned to the strangers. "I suppose these are the earth folks you were expecting?"

"Yes," returned the Queen; "the girl is named Mayre, and the man Cap'n Bill."

While the sea serpent looked at the visitors they ventured to look at him. He certainly was a queer creature, yet Trot decided he was not at all frightful. His head was round as a ball, but his ears were sharp pointed and had tassels at the ends of them. His nose was flat and his mouth very wide indeed, but his eyes were blue and gentle in expression. The white, stubby hairs that surrounded his face were not thick, like a beard, but scattered and scraggly. From the head, the long brown body of the sea serpent extended to the hole in the coral wall, which was just big enough to admit it, and how much more of the body remained outside the child could not tell. On the back of the body were several fins, which made the creature look more like an eel than a serpent.

"The girl is young and the man is old," said King Anko, in a soft voice. "But I'm quite sure Cap'n Bill isn't as old as I am."

"How old are you?" asked the sailor.

"I can't say, exactly. I can remember several thousands of years back, but beyond that my memory fails me. How's your memory, Cap'n Bill?"

"You've got me beat," was the reply. "I'll give in that you're older than I am."

This seemed to please the sea serpent.

"Are you well?" he asked.

"Pretty fair," said Cap'n Bill. "How's yourself?"

"Oh, I'm very well, thank you," answered Anko. "I never remember to have had a pain but three times in my life. The last time was when Julius Sneezer was on earth."

"You mean Julius Cæsar," said Trot, correcting him.

"No; I mean Julius Sneezer," insisted the Sea Serpent.

"That was his real name—Sneezer. They called him Cæsar sometimes, just because he took everything he could lay hands on. I ought to know, because I saw him when he was alive. Did you see him when he was alive, Cap'n Bill?"

"I reckon not," admitted the sailor.

"That time I had a toothache," continued Anko; "but I got a lobster to pull the tooth with his claw, so the pain was soon over."

"Did it hurt to pull it?" asked Trot.

"Hurt!" exclaimed the Sea Serpent, groaning at the recollection. "My dear, those creatures have been called lobsters ever since! The second pain I had way back in the time of Nevercouldnever."

"Oh, I s'pose you mean Nebuchadnezzar," said Trot.

"Do you call him that, now?" asked the Sea Serpent, as if surprised. "He used to be called Nevercouldnever when he was alive, but this new way of spelling seems to get everything mixed up. Nebuchadnezzar does n't mean anything at all, it seems to me."

"It means he ate grass," said the child.

"Oh, no; he did n't," declared the Sea Serpent. "He was the first to discover that lettuce was good to eat, and he became very fond of it. The people may have called it grass, but they were wrong. I ought to know, because I was alive when Nevercouldnever lived. Were you alive, then?"

"No," said Trot.

"The pain I had then," remarked Anko, "was caused by a kink in my tail, about three hundred feet from the end. There was an old octopus who did not like me, and so he tied a knot in my tail when I was n't looking."

"What did you do?" asked Cap'n Bill.

"Well, first I transformed the octopus into a jelly fish, and then I waited for the tide to turn. When my tail was untied the pain stopped."

"I—I don't understand that," said Trot, somewhat bewildered.

"Thank you, my dear," replied the Sea Serpent, in a grateful voice. "People who are always understood are very common. You are sure to respect those you can't understand, for you feel that perhaps they know more than you do."

"About how long do you happen to be?" inquired Cap'n Bill.

"When last measured, I was seven thousand four hundred and eighty-two feet, five inches and a quarter. I 'm not sure about the quarter, but the rest is probably correct. Adam measured me when Cain was a baby."

"Where 's the rest of you, then?" asked Trot.

"Safe at home, I hope, and coiled up in my parlor," answered the Sea Serpent. "When I go out I usually take along only what is needed. It saves a lot of bother and I can always find my way back in the darkest night, by just coiling up the part that has been away."

"Do you like to be a sea serpent?" inquired the child.

"Yes, for I'm King of my Ocean, and there is no other sea serpent to imagine he is just as good as I am. I have two brothers who live in other oceans, but one is seven inches shorter than I am, and the other several feet shorter. It's

curious to talk about feet when we have n't any feet, is n't it?"

"Seems so," acknowledged Trot.

"I feel I have much to be proud of," continued Anko, in a dreamy tone; "my great age, my undisputed sway, and my exceptional length."

Chapter Five

"I don't b'lieve I 'd care to live so long," remarked Cap'n Bill, thoughtfully.

"So long as seven thousand four hundred and eighty-two feet, five inches and a quarter?" asked the Sea Serpent.

"No; I mean so many years," replied the sailor.

"But what can one do, if one happens to be a sea serpent?" Anko inquired. "There is nothing in the sea that can hurt me, and I cannot commit suicide because we have no carbolic acid, or firearms, or gas to turn on. So it is n't a matter of choice, and I 'd about as soon be alive as dead. It does not seem quite so monotonous, you know. But I guess I 've stayed about long enough; so I 'll go home to dinner. Come and see me, when you have time."

"Thank you," said Trot; and Merla added:

"I 'll take you over to his majesty's palace when we go out, and let you see how he lives."

"Yes, do," said Anko; and then he slowly slid out of the hole, which immediately closed behind him, leaving the coral wall as solid as before.

"Oh!" exclaimed Trot; "King Anko forgot to tell us what the third pain was about."

"So he did," said Cap'n Bill. "We must ask him about that, when we see him. But I guess the ol' boy's mem'ry is failin', an' he can't be depended on for pertic'lars."

EXPLORING THE OCEAN

Chap. 6.

THE queen now requested her guests to recline upon couches, that they might rest themselves from their long swim and talk more at their ease. So the girl and the sailor allowed themselves to float downward until they rested their bodies on two of the couches nearest the throne, which were willingly vacated for them by the mermaids who had occupied them until then.

The visitors soon found themselves answering a great many questions about their life on the earth, for, although the queen had said she kept track of what was going on on the land, there were many details of human life in which all the mermaids seemed greatly interested.

During the conversation several sea-maids came swimming into the room, bearing trays of sea apples and other fruit, which they first offered to the queen and then passed the refreshments around to the company assembled. Trot and Cap'n Bill each took some, and the little girl found the fruits delicious to eat, as they had a richer flavor than any that grew upon land. Queen Aquareine was much pleased when the old sailor asked for more, but Merla warned him dinner would soon be served and he must take care not to spoil his appetite for that meal.

"Our dinner is at noon, for we have to cook in the middle of the day, when the sun is shining," she said.

"Cook!" cried Trot; "why, you can't build a fire in the water, can you?"

"We have no need of fires," was the reply. "The glass roof of our kitchen is so curved that it concentrates the heat of the sun's rays, which are then hot enough to cook anything we wish."

"But how do you get along if the day is cloudy, and the sun does n't shine?" inquired the little girl.

"Then we use the hot springs that bubble up in another part of the palace," Merla answered. "But the sun is the best to cook by."

So, it was no surprise to Trot when, about noon, dinner was announced and all the mermaids, headed by their queen and their guests, swam into another spacious room where a great, long table was laid. The dishes were of polished gold and dainty cut glass, and the cloth and napkins of fine gossamer. Around the table were ranged rows of couches for the mermaids to recline upon as they ate. Only the nobility and favorites of Queen Aquareine were invited to partake of this repast, for Clia explained that tables were set for the other mermaids in different parts of the numerous palaces.

Trot wondered who would serve the meal, but her curiosity was soon satisfied when several large lobsters came sliding into the room, backward, bearing in their claws trays loaded with food. Each of these lobsters had a golden band around its neck to show it was the slave of the mermaids.

These curious waiters were fussy creatures and Trot found

much amusement in watching their odd motions. They were so spry and excitable that, at times, they ran against one another and upset the platters of food, after which they began to scold and argue as to whose fault it was, until one of the mermaids quietly rebuked them and asked them to be more quiet and more careful.

The queen's guests had no cause to complain of the dinner provided. First the lobsters served bowls of turtle soup, which proved hot and deliciously flavored. Then came salmon steaks fried in fish oil, with a fungus bread that tasted much like field mushrooms. Oysters, clams, soft-shell crabs and various preparations of sea foods followed. The salad was a delicate leaf from some seaweed that Trot thought was much nicer than lettuce. Several courses were served and the lobsters changed the plates with each course, chattering and scolding as they worked, and as Trot said, "doing everything backwards" in their nervous, fussy way.

Many of the things offered them to eat were unknown to the visitors, and the child was suspicious of some of them; but Cap'n Bill asked no questions and ate everything offered him, so Trot decided to follow his example. Certain it is they found the meal very satisfying, and evidently there was no danger of their being hungry while they remained the guests of the mermaids. When the fruits came, Trot thought that must be the last course of the big dinner, but, following the fruits were ice creams frozen into the shapes of flowers.

"How funny," said the child, "to be eating ice cream at the bottom of the sea!"

"Why does that surprise you?" inquired the Queen.

"I can't see where you get the ice to freeze it," Trot replied.

"It is brought to us from the icebergs that float in the northern parts of the ocean," explained Merla.

"O' course, Trot; you orter thought o' that; I did," said Cap'n Bill.

The little girl was glad there was no more to eat, for she was ashamed to feel she had eaten every morsel she could. Her only excuse for being so greedy was that "ev'rything tasted just splendid!" as she told the queen.

"And now," said Aquareine, "I will send you out for a swim with Merla, who will show you some of the curious sights of our sea. You need not go far this afternoon, and when you return we will have another interesting talk together."

So the blonde mermaid led Trot and Cap'n Bill outside the palace walls, where they found themselves in the pretty flower gardens.

"I'd feel all right, mate, if I could have a smoke," remarked the old sailor to the child; "but that's a thing as can't be did here in the water."

"Why not?" asked Merla, who overheard him.

"A pipe has to be lighted, an' a match would n't burn," he replied.

"Try it," suggested the mermaid. "I do not mind your smoking at all, if it will give you pleasure."

"It's a bad habit I 've got, an' I 'm too old to break myself of it," said Cap'n Bill. Then he felt in the big pockets of his coat and took out a pipe and a bag of tobacco. After he had carefully filled his pipe, rejoicing in the fact that the tobacco was not at all wet, he took out his match box and struck a light. The match burned brightly and soon the sailor was puffing the smoke from his pipe in great contentment. The smoke ascended through the water in the shape of bubbles and Trot wondered what anyone who happened to be floating upon the surface of the ocean would think to see smoke coming from the water.

"Well, I find I can smoke, all right," remarked Cap'n Bill; "but it bothers me to understand why."

"It is because of the air space existing between the water and everything you have about you," explained Merla. "But now, if you will come this way, I will take you to visit some of our neighbors."

They passed over the carpet of sea flowers, the gorgeous

blossoms swaying on their stems as the motion of the people in the water above them disturbed their repose, and presently the three entered the dense shrubbery surrounding the palaces. They had not proceeded far when they came to a clearing among the bushes, and here Merla paused.

Trot and Cap'n Bill paused, too, for floating in the clear water was a group of beautiful shapes that the child thought looked like molds of wine jelly. They were round as a dinner plate, soft and transparent, but tinted in such lovely hues that no artist's brush has ever been able to imitate them. Some were deep sapphire blue; others rose pink; still others a delicate topaz color. They seemed to have neither heads, eyes nor ears, yet it was easy to see they were alive and able to float in any direction they wished to go. In shape they resembled inverted flowerpots, with the upper edges fluted, and from the centers floated what seemed to be bouquets of flowers.

"How pretty!" exclaimed Trot, enraptured by the sight.

"Yes; this is a rare variety of jellyfish," replied Merla. "The creatures are not so delicate as they appear, and live for a long time—unless they get too near the surface and the waves wash them ashore."

After watching the jellyfish a few moments they followed Merla through the grove and soon a low chant, like that of an Indian song, fell upon their ears. It was a chorus of many small voices, and grew louder as they swam on. Presently a big rock rose suddenly before them from the bottom of the sea, rearing its steep side far up into the water overhead, and this rock was thickly covered with tiny shells that clung fast to its surface. The chorus they heard appeared to come from these shells, and Merla said to her companions:

"These are the singing barnacles. They are really very amusing, and if you listen carefully you can hear what they say."

So Trot and Cap'n Bill listened, and this was what the barnacles sang:

"We went to topsy-turvy land to see a man-o'-war,
And we were much attached to it, because we simply were;
We found an anchor-ite within the mud upon the lea
For the ghost of Jonah's whale he ran away and went to sea.
　　　　Oh, it was awful!
　　　　It was unlawful!
We rallied round the flag in sev'ral millions;
　　　　They could n't shake us;
　　　　They had to take us;
So the halibut and cod they danced cotillions."

"What does it all mean?" asked Trot.

"I suppose they refer to the way barnacles have of clinging to ships," replied Merla; "but usually their songs mean nothing at all. The little barnacles have n't many brains, so we usually find their songs quite stupid."

"Do they write comic operas?" asked the child.

"I think not," answered the mermaid.

"They seem to like the songs themselves," remarked Cap'n Bill.

"Oh, yes; they sing all day long. But it never matters to them whether their songs mean anything or not. Let us go in this direction and visit some other sea people."

So they swam away from the barnacle-covered rock and Trot heard the last chorus as she slowly followed their conductor. The barnacles were singing:

> *"Oh, very well, then,*
> *I hear the curfew,*
> *Please go away and come some other day;*
> *Goliath tussels*
> *With Samson's muscles,*
> *Yet the muscles never fight in Oyster Bay."*

"It 's jus' nonsense!" said Trot, scornfully. "Why don't they sing 'Annie Laurie,' or 'Home, Sweet Home,' or else keep quiet?"

"Why, if they were quiet," replied Merla, "they would n't be singing barnacles."

71

Chapter Six

They now came to one of the avenues which led from the sea garden out into the broad ocean, and here two swordfishes were standing guard.

"Is all quiet?" Merla asked them.

"Just as usual, your Highness," replied one of the guards. "Mummercubble was sick this morning, and grunted dreadfully; but he's better now and has gone to sleep. King Anko has been stirring around some, but is now taking his after-dinner nap. I think it will be perfectly safe for you to swim out for a while, if you wish."

"Who's Mummercubble?" asked Trot, as they passed out into deep water.

"He's the sea pig," replied Merla. "I am glad he is asleep, for now we won't meet him."

"Don't you like him?" inquired Trot.

"Oh, he complains so bitterly of everything that he bores us," Merla answered. "Mummercubble is never contented or happy for a single minute."

"I've seen people like that," said Cap'n Bill, with a nod of his head; "an' they has a way of upsettin' the happiest folks they meet."

"Look out!" suddenly cried the mermaid. "Look out for your fingers! Here are the snapping eels."

"Who? Where?" asked Trot, anxiously.

And now, they were in the midst of a cluster of wriggling,

darting eels which sported all around them in the water with marvelous activity.

"Yes, look out for your fingers and your noses!" said one of the eels, making a dash for Cap'n Bill. At first the sailor was tempted to put out a hand and push the creature away, but remembering that his fingers would thus be exposed he

remained quiet, and the eel snapped harmlessly just before his face, and then darted away.

"Stop it!" said Merla; "stop it this minute, or I'll report your impudence to Aquareine."

"Oh, who cares?" shouted the Eels. "We're not afraid of the mermaids."

The Sea Fairies

"She 'll stiffen you all up again, as she did once before," said Merla, "if you try to hurt the earth people."

"Are these earth people?" asked one. And then they all stopped their play and regarded Trot and Cap'n Bill with their little black eyes.

"The old polliwog looks something like King Anko," said one of them.

"I 'm not a polliwog!" answered Cap'n Bill, angrily. "I 'm a re-spec'able sailorman, an' I 'll have you treat me decent or I 'll know why.

"Sailor!" said another. "That means to float on the water—not *in* it. What are you doing down here?"

"I'm jes' a-visitin'," answered Cap'n Bill.

"He is the guest of our queen," said Merla, "and so is this little girl. If you do not behave nicely to them you will surely be sorry."

"Oh, that 's all right," replied one of the biggest eels, wriggling around in a circle and then snapping at a companion, which as quickly snapped out of his way. "We know how to be polite to company as well as the mermaids. We won't hurt them."

"Come on, fellows; let 's go scare old Mummercubble," cried another; and then in a flash, they all darted away and left our friends to themselves.

Trot was greatly relieved.

74

Chapter Six

"I don't like eels," she said.

"They are more mischievous than harmful," replied Merla; "but I do not care much for them myself."

"No," added Cap'n Bill; "they ain't respec'ful."

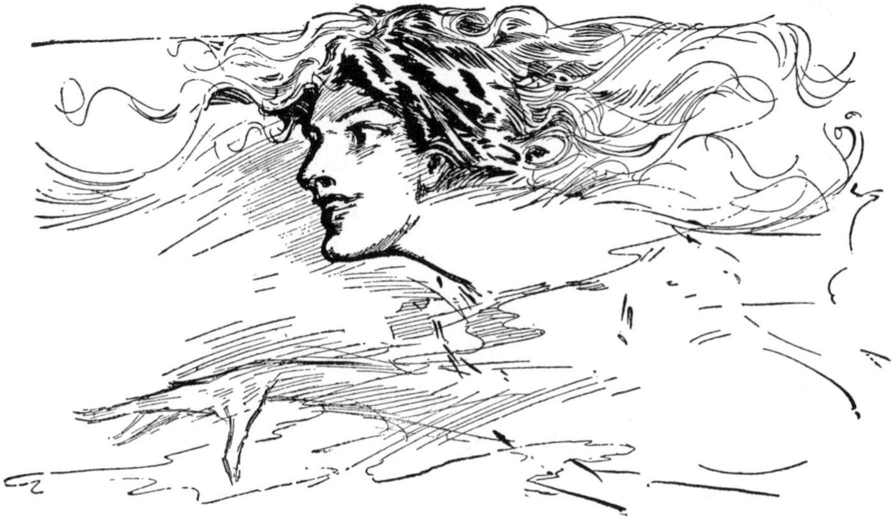

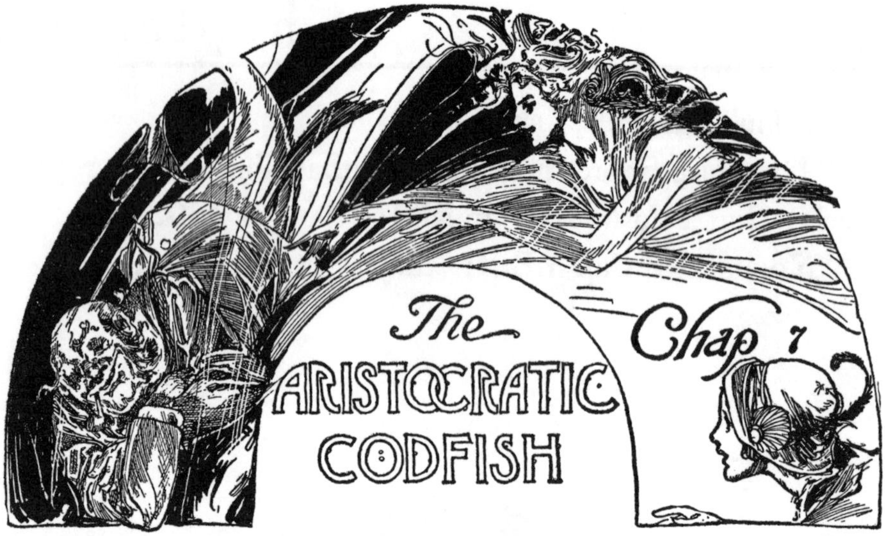
Chap 7
The
ARISTOCRATIC
CODFISH

THE three swam slowly along, quite enjoying the cool depths of the water. Every little while they met with some strange creature—or one that seemed strange to the earth people—for although Trot and Cap'n Bill had seen many kinds of fish, after they had been caught and pulled from the water, that was very different from meeting them in their own element, "face to face," as Trot expressed it. Now that the various fishes were swimming around free and unafraid in their deep-sea home, they were quite different from the gasping, excited creatures struggling at the end of a fishline, or flopping from a net.

Before long they came upon a group of large fishes lying lazily near the bottom of the sea. They were a dark color upon their backs and silver underneath, but not especially pretty to look at. The fishes made no effort to get out of

Merla's way and remained motionless, except for the gentle motion of their fins and gills.

"Here," said the mermaid, pausing, "is the most aristocratic family of fish in all the sea."

"What are they?" asked the girl.

"Codfish," was the reply. "Their only fault is that they are too haughty and foolishly proud of their pedigree."

Overhearing this speech one codfish said to another, in a very dignified tone of voice: "What insolence!"

"Isn't it?" replied the other. "There ought to be a law to prevent these common mermaids from discussing their superiors."

"My sakes!" said Trot, astonished; "how stuck up they are, aren't they?"

For a moment the group of fishes stared at her solemnly. Then one of them remarked in a disdainful manner:

"Come, my dears, let us leave these vulgar creatures."

"I'm not as vulgar as you are!" exclaimed Trot, much offended by this speech. "Where I came from we only eat codfish when there's nothing else in the house to eat."

"How absurd!" observed one of the creatures, arrogantly.

"Eat codfish, indeed!" said another in a lofty manner.

"Yes, and you're pretty salty, too, I can tell you. At home you're nothing but a pick-up!" said Trot.

"Dear me!" exclaimed the first fish which had spoken;

"must we stand this insulting language—and from a person to whom we have never been introduced?"

"I don't need any interduction," replied the girl; "I've eaten you, and you always make me thirsty."

Merla laughed merrily at this, and the codfish said, with much dignity:

"Come, fellow aristocrats; let us go."

"Never mind; we're going ourselves," announced Merla, and followed by her guests the pretty mermaid swam away.

"I've heard tell of codfish aristocercy," said Cap'n Bill; "but I never knowed 'zac'ly what it meant afore."

"They jus' made me mad, with all their airs," observed Trot; "so I gave 'em a piece of my mind."

"You surely did, mate," said the sailor; "but I ain't sure they understand what they're like when they're salted an' hung up in the pantry. Folks gener'ly gets stuck-up 'cause they don't know theirselves like other folks knows 'em."

"We are near Crabville now," declared Merla. "Shall we visit the crabs and see what they are doing?"

"Yes, let's," replied Trot. "The crabs are lots of fun. I've often caught them among the rocks on the shore and laughed at the way they act. Was n't it funny at dinner time to see the way they slid around with the plates?"

"Those were not crabs, but lobsters and crawfish," remarked the mermaid. "They are very intelligent creatures,

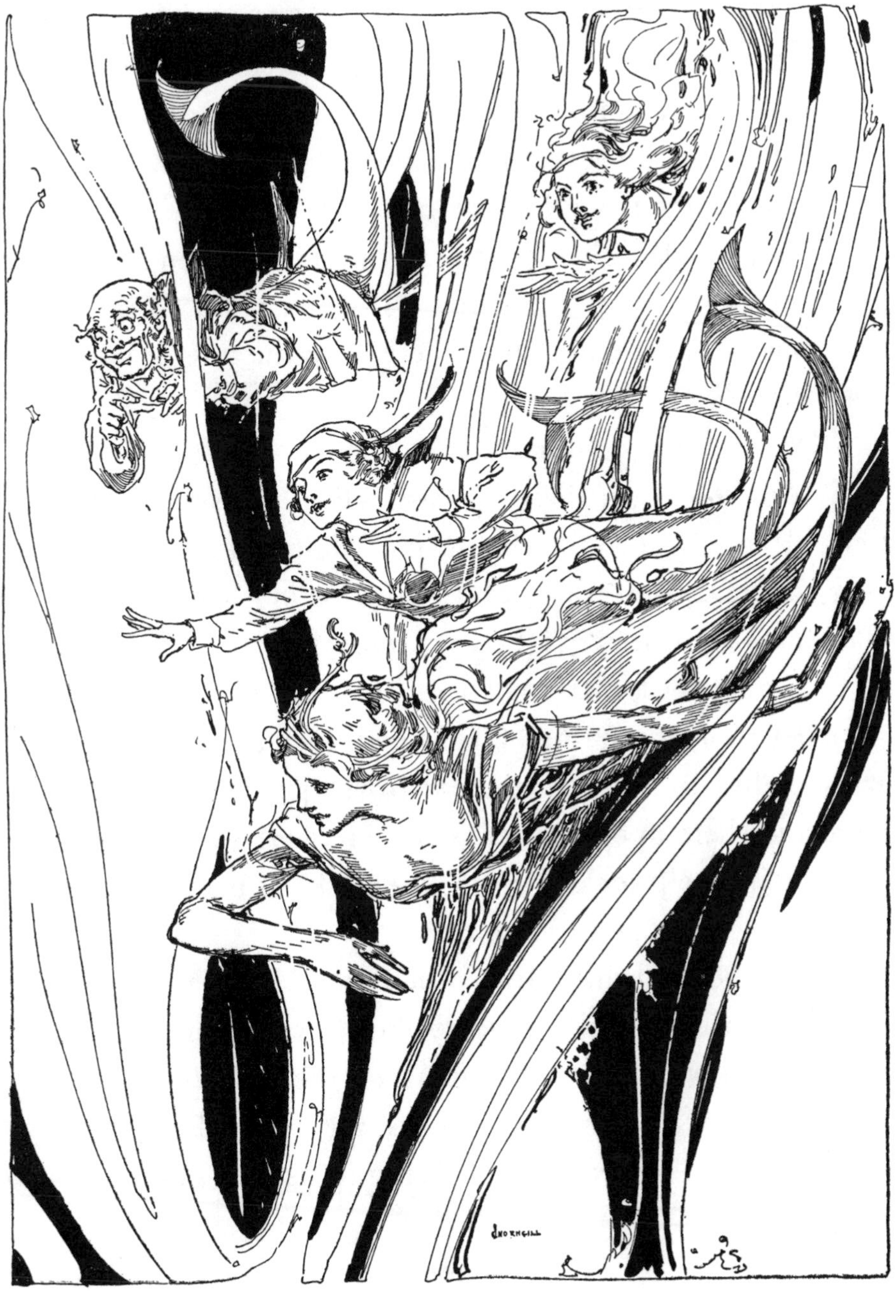

and by making them serve us we save ourselves much household work. Of course, they are awkward and provoke us sometimes; but no servants are perfect, it is said, so we get along with ours as well as we can."

"They're all right," protested the child, "even if they did tip things over once in a while. But it is easy to work in a sea palace, I'm sure, because there's no dusting or sweeping to be done."

"Or scrubbin'," added Cap'n Bill.

"The crabs," said Merla, "are second cousins to the lobsters, although much smaller in size. There are many families —or varieties—of crabs, and so many of them live in one place near here that we call it Crabville. I think you will enjoy seeing these little creatures in their native haunts."

They now approached a kelp bed, the straight, thin stems of the kelp running far upward to the surface of the water. Here and there upon the stalks were leaves, but Trot thought the growing kelp looked much like sticks of macaroni, except they were a rich, red-brown color.

It was beyond the kelp—which they had to push aside as they swam through it, so thickly did it grow—that they came to a higher level, a sort of plateau on the ocean's bottom. It was covered with scattered rocks of all sizes, which appeared to have broken off from big shelving rocks they observed near

by. The place they entered seemed like one of the rocky
canyons you often see upon the earth.

"Here live the fiddler crabs," said Merla; "but we must
have taken them by surprise, it is so quiet."

Even as she spoke there was a stirring and scrambling
among the rocks, and soon scores of light green crabs were
gathered before the visitors. The crabs bore fiddles of all
sorts and shapes in their claws, and one big fellow carried a
leader's baton. The latter crab climbed upon a flat rock and
in an excited voice called out:

"Ready, now—ready, good fiddlers. We'll play Number 19—Hail to the Mermaids. Ready! Take aim! Fire
away!"

At this command every crab began scraping at his fiddle
as hard as he could, and the sounds were so shrill and un-
musical that Trot wondered when they would begin to play
a tune. But they never did; it was one regular mix-up of
sounds from beginning to end. When the noise finally
stopped the leader turned to his visitors and, waving his
baton toward them, asked:

"Well, what do you think of that?"

"Not much," said Trot, honestly. "What's it all about?"

"I composed it myself!" said the Fiddler Crab. "But it's
highly classical, I admit. All really great music is an ac-
quired taste."

The Sea Fairies

"I don't like it," remarked Cap'n Bill. "It might do all right to stir up a racket New Year's Eve, but to call that screechin' music—"

Just then the crabs started fiddling again, harder than ever, and as it promised to be a long performance they left the little creatures scraping away at their fiddles, as if for dear life, and swam along the rocky canyon until, on turning a corner, they came upon a new and different scene.

There were crabs here, too—many of them—and they were performing the queerest antics imaginable. Some were building themselves into a pyramid, each standing on edge, with the biggest and strongest ones at the bottom. When the crabs were five or six rows high they would all tumble over, still clinging to one another, and, having reached the ground, they would separate and commence to build the pyramid over again.

Others were chasing one another around in a circle, always moving backward or sidewise, and trying to play "leapfrog" as they went. Still others were swinging on slight branches of seaweed, or turning cart wheels, or indulging in similar antics.

Merla and the earth people watched the busy little creatures for some time before they were themselves observed; but finally, Trot gave a laugh when one crab fell on its back and began frantically waving its legs to get right-side-up again.

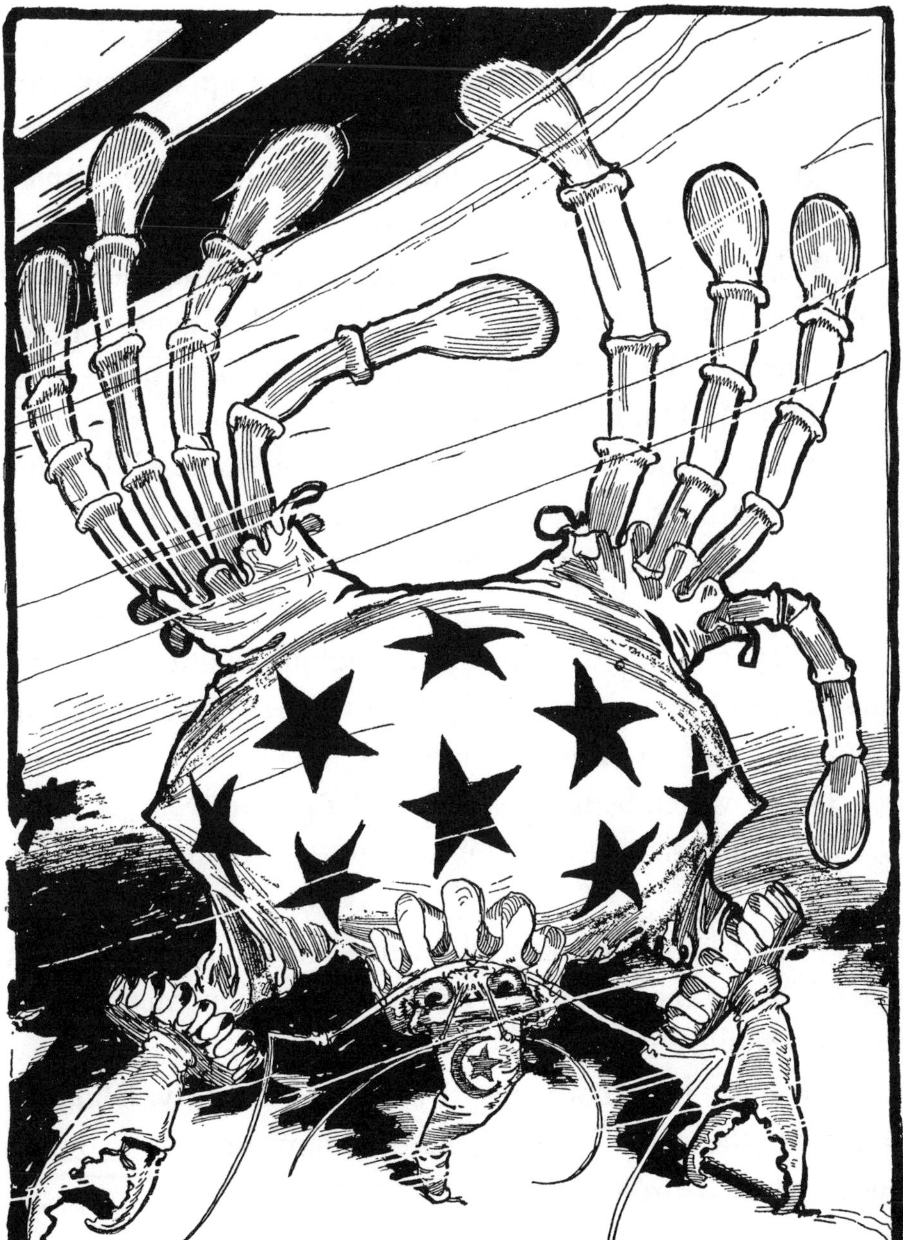

The Sea Fairies

At the sound of her laughter they all stopped their play and came toward the visitors in a flock, looking up at them with their bright eyes in a most comical way.

"Welcome home!" cried one, as he turned a back somersault and knocked another crab over.

"What's the difference between a mermaid and a tadpole?" asked another, in a loud voice, and without a pause continued: "why, one drops its tail and the other holds on to it. Ha, ha! Ho, ho! Hee-hee!"

"These," said Merla, "are the clown crabs. They are very silly things, as you may already have discovered; but for a short time they are rather amusing. One tires of them very soon."

"They're funny," said Trot, laughing again. "It's almost as good as a circus. I don't think they would make me tired; but, then, I'm not a mermaid."

The clown crabs had now formed a row in front of them.

"Mr. Johnsing," asked one, "why is a mermaid like an automobile?"

"I don't know, Tommy Blimken," answered a big crab in the middle of the row. "*Why* do you think a mermaid is like an automobile?"

"Because they both get tired," said Tommy Blimken. Then all the crabs laughed, and Tommy seemed to laugh louder than the rest.

"How do the crabs in the sea know anything 'bout auto-'biles?" asked Trot.

"Why, Tommy Blimken and Harry Hustle were both captured once by humans and put in an aquarium," answered the mermaid. "But one day they climbed out and escaped, finally making their way back to the sea and home again. So they are quite traveled you see, and great favorites among the crabs. While they were on land they saw a great many curious things, and so I suppose they saw automobiles."

"We did, we did!" cried Harry Hustle, an awkward crab with one big claw and one little one. "And we saw earth people with legs—awfully funny they were; and animals called horses, with legs; and other creatures with legs; and the people cover themselves with the queerest things—they even wear feathers and flowers on their heads, and——"

"Oh, we know all about that," said Trot; "we live on the earth ourselves."

"Well, you're lucky to get off from it and into the good water," said the Crab. "I nearly died on the earth; it was so stupid, dry and airy. But the circus was great. They held the performance right in front of the aquarium where we lived, and Tommy and I learned all the tricks of the tumblers. Hi! Come on, fellows, and show the earth people what you can do!"

At this the crabs began performing their antics again; but

they did the same things over and over, so Cap'n Bill and Trot soon tired, as Merla said they would, and decided they had seen enough of the crab circus. So they proceeded to swim farther up the rocky canyon, and near its upper end they came to a lot of conch shells lying upon the sandy bottom. A funny looking crab was sticking his head out from each of these shells.

"Here are the hermit crabs," said one of the mermaids. "They steal these shells and live in them, so no enemies can attack them."

"Don't they get lonesome?" asked Trot.

"Perhaps so, my dear. But they do not seem to mind being lonesome. They are great cowards, and think if they can but protect their lives there is nothing else to care for. Unlike the jolly crabs we have just left, the hermits are cross and unsociable."

"Oh, keep quiet and go away!" said one of the hermit crabs, in a grumpy voice. "No one wants mermaids around here." Then every crab withdrew its head into its shell, and our friends saw them no more.

"They're not very polite," observed Trot, following the mermaid as Merla swam upward into the middle water.

"I know, now, why cross people are called 'crabbed'," said Cap'n Bill. "They've got dispositions jes' like these 'ere hermit crabs."

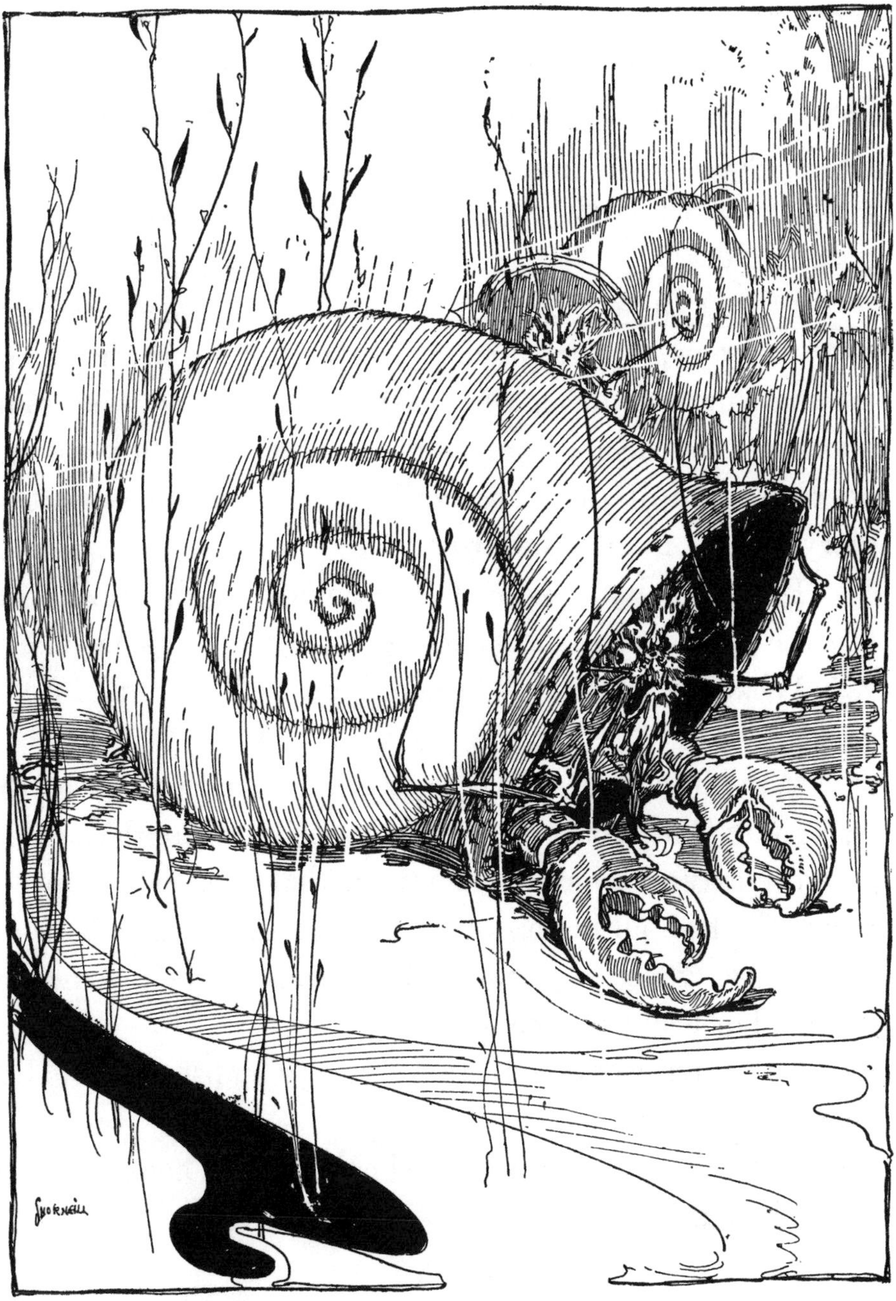

The Sea Fairies

Presently, they came upon a small flock of mackerel, and noticed that the fishes seemed much excited. When they saw the mermaid they cried out:

"Oh, Merla! what do you think? Our Flippity has just gone to glory!"

"When?" asked the mermaid.

"Just now," one replied. "We were lying in the water, talking quietly together when a spinning, shining thing came along and our dear Flippity ate it. Then he went shooting up to the top of the water and gave a flop and—went to glory! Isn't it splendid, Merla?"

"Poor Flippity!" sighed the mermaid. "I'm sorry, for he was the prettiest and nicest mackerel in your whole flock."

"What does it mean?" asked Trot. "How did Flippity go to glory?"

"Why, he was caught by a hook, and pulled out of the water into some boat," Merla explained. "But these poor, stupid creatures do not understand that; and when one of them is jerked out of the water and disappears they have an idea he has gone to glory—which means to them some unknown, but beautiful sea."

"I've often wondered," said Trot, "why fishes are foolish enough to bite on hooks."

"They must know enough to know they're hooks," added Cap'n Bill, musingly.

Chapter Seven

"Oh, they do," replied Merla. "I've seen fishes gather around a hook and look at it carefully for a long time. They well know it is a hook, and that if they bite the bait upon it they will be pulled out of the water. But they are curious to know what will happen to them afterward, and think it means happiness, instead of death. So finally, one takes the hook and disappears, and the others never know what becomes of him."

"Why don't you tell 'em the truth?" asked Trot.

"Oh, we do. The mermaids have warned them many times, but it does no good at all. The fish are stupid creatures."

"But I wish I was Flippity," said one of the mackerel, staring at Trot with his big, round eyes. "He went to glory before I could eat the hook myself."

"You're lucky," answered the child. "Flippity will be fried in a pan for some one's dinner. You wouldn't like that, would you?"

"Flippity has gone to glory!" said another, and then they swam away in haste to tell the news to all they met.

"I never heard of anything so foolish," remarked Trot, as they swam slowly on through the clear blue water.

"Yes; it is very foolish, and very sad," answered Merla. "But, if the fishes were wise, men could not catch them for food, and many poor people on your earth make their living by fishing."

"It seems wicked to catch such pretty things," said the child.

"I do not think so," Merla replied, laughingly; "for they were born to become food for some one, and men are not the only ones that eat fishes. Many creatures of the sea feed upon them. They even eat one another, at times. And if none was ever destroyed they would soon become so numerous that they would clog the waters of the ocean, and leave no room for the rest of us. So, after all, perhaps it is just as well they are thoughtless and foolish."

Presently they came to some round balls that looked much like balloons in shape and were gaily colored. They floated quietly in the water, and Trot inquired what they were.

"Balloonfish," answered Merla. "They are helpless creatures, but have little spikes all over them, so their enemies dare not bite them for fear of getting pricked."

Trot found the balloonfish quite interesting. They had little dots of eyes and dots for mouths; but she could see no noses, and their fins and tails were very small.

"They catch these fish in the South Sea Islands and make lanterns of 'em," said Cap'n Bill. "They first skin 'em, and sew the skin up again to let it dry, and then they put candles inside and the light shines through the dried skin."

Chapter Seven

Many other curious sights they saw in the ocean that afternoon, and both Cap'n Bill and Trot thoroughly enjoyed their glimpse of sea life. At last Merla said it was time to return to the palace, from which she claimed they had not, at any time, been very far distant.

"We must prepare for dinner, as it will soon begin to grow dark in the water," continued their conductor. So they swam leisurely back to the groves that surrounded the palaces, and as they entered the gardens the sun sank, and deep shadows began to form in the ocean depths.

A BANQUET UNDER WATER

Chap. 8.

THE palaces of the mermaids were all aglow with lights as they approached them, and Trot was amazed at the sight.

"Where did the lamps come from?" she asked their guide, wonderingly.

"They are not lamps, my dear," replied Merla, much amused at this suggestion; "we use electric lights in our palaces, and have done so for thousands of years—long before the earth people knew of electric lights."

"But where do you get 'em?" inquired Cap'n Bill, who was as much astonished as the girl.

"From a transparent jellyfish which naturally emits a strong and beautiful electric light," was the answer. "We have many hundreds of them in our palaces, as you will presently see."

Their way was now lighted by small phosphorescent

creatures scattered about the sea gardens and which Merla informed them were hyalæa, or sea glowworms. But their light was dim when compared to that of the electric jellyfish, which they found placed in clusters upon the ceilings of all the rooms of the palaces, rendering them light as day.

Trot watched these curious creatures with delight, for delicately colored lights ran around their bodies in every direction in a continuous stream, shedding splendid rays throughout the vast halls.

A group of mermaids met the visitors in the hall of the main palace, and told Merla the queen had instructed them to show the guests to their rooms as soon as they arrived. So Trot followed two of them through several passages, after which they swam upward and entered a circular opening. There were no stairs here, because there was no need of them, and the little girl soon found herself in an upper room that was very beautiful indeed.

All the walls were covered with iridescent shells, polished till they resembled mother-of-pearl, and upon the glass ceiling were clusters of the brilliant electric jellyfish, rendering the room bright and cheerful with their radiance. In one corner stood a couch of white coral, with gossamer draperies floating around it from the four high posts. Upon examining it, the child found the couch was covered with soft, amber sponges, which rendered it very comfortable to lie upon. In a wardrobe she found several beautiful gossamer gowns, richly embroidered in colored seaweeds, and these Mayre was told she might wear while she remained the guest of the mermaids. She also found a toilet table with brushes, combs and other conveniences, all of which were made of polished tortoise-shell.

Really, the room was more dainty and comfortable than one might suppose possible in a palace far beneath the surface of the sea, and Trot was greatly delighted with her new quarters.

The mermaid attendants assisted the child to dress herself in one of the prettiest robes, which she found to be quite dry and fitted perfectly. Then the sea-maids brushed and dressed her hair, and tied it with ribbons of cherry-red seaweed. Finally they placed around her neck a string of pearls that would have been priceless upon the earth, and now the little girl announced she was ready for supper and had a good appetite.

Cap'n Bill had been given a similar room, near Trot's; but the old sailor refused to change his clothes for any others offered him, for which reason he was ready for supper long before his comrade.

"What bothers me, mate," he said to the little girl, as they swam toward the great banquet hall where Queen Aquareine awaited them, "is why we ain't crushed by the pressin' of the water agin us, bein' as we 're down here in the deep sea."

"How 's that, Cap'n? Why should we be crushed?" she asked.

"Why, ev'r'body knows that the deeper you go in the sea the more the water presses agin you," he explained. "Even the divers in their steel jackets can't stand it very deep down. An' here we be, miles from the top o' the water, I 'spect, an' we don't feel crowded a bit."

"I know why," answered the child, wisely. "The water don't touch us, you see. If it did, it might crush us; but it don't. It 's always held a little way off from our bodies by the magic of the fairy mermaids."

"True enough, Trot," declared the sailorman. "What an idjut I was not to think o' that myself!"

In the royal banquet hall were assembled many of the mermaids, headed by the lovely queen, and as soon as their earth guests arrived Aquareine ordered the meal to be served.

The lobsters again waited upon the table, wearing little white caps and aprons which made them look very funny; but Trot was so hungry after her afternoon's excursion that she did not pay as much attention to the lobsters as she did to her supper, which was very delicious and consisted of many courses. A lobster spilled some soup on Cap'n Bill's bald head and made him yell for a minute, because it was hot and he had not expected it, but the queen apologized very sweetly for the awkwardness of her servants, and the sailor soon forgot all about the incident in his enjoyment of the meal.

After the feast ended they all went to the big reception room, where some of the mermaids played upon harps while others sang pretty songs. They danced together, too—a graceful swimming-dance, so queer to the little girl that it interested and amused her greatly.

Cap'n Bill seemed a bit bashful among so many beautiful mermaids, yet he was pleased when the queen offered him a place beside her throne, where he could see and hear all the delightful entertainment provided for the royal guests. He did not talk much, being a man of few words except when alone with Trot; but his light blue eyes were big and round with wonder at the sights he saw.

Trot and the sailorman went to bed early and slept soundly upon their sponge-covered couches. The little girl never wakened until long after the sun was shining down through the glass roof of her room, and when she opened her eyes she was startled to find a number of big, small and middle-sized fishes staring at her through the glass.

"That's one bad thing 'bout this mermaid palace," she said to herself; "it's too public. Ever'thing in the sea can look at you through the glass as much as it likes. I would n't mind fishes looking at me if they had n't such big eyes, an'—

goodness me! There's a monster that's all head! And there goes a fish with a sail on its back; an' here's old Mummercubble, I'm sure, for he's got a head just like a pig."

She might have watched the fishes on the roof for hours, had she not remembered it was late and breakfast must be

ready. So she dressed, and made her toilet, and swam down into the palace to find Cap'n Bill and the mermaids politely waiting for her to join them.

The sea maidens were as fresh and lovely as ever, while each and all proved sweet tempered and merry, even at the breakfast table—and that is where people are cross, if they ever are. During the meal the queen said:

"I shall take you this morning to the most interesting part of the ocean, where the largest and most remarkable sea creatures live. And we must visit King Anko, too, for the sea serpent would feel hurt and slighted if I did not bring my guests to call upon him."

"That will be nice," said Trot, eagerly; but Cap'n Bill asked:

"Is there any danger, ma'am?"

"I think not," replied Queen Aquareine. "I cannot see that you will be exposed to any danger at all, so long as I am with you. But we are going into the neighborhood of some fierce and even terrible beings, which would attack you at once did they suspect you to be earth people. So, in order to guard your safety, I intend to draw the Magic Circle around both of you before we start."

"What is the Magic Circle?" asked Trot.

"A fairy charm that prevents any enemy from touching you. No monster of the sea, however powerful, will be able to reach your body while you are protected by the Magic Circle," declared the Queen.

"Oh, then, I'll not be a bit afraid," returned the child, with perfect confidence.

Chapter Eight

"Am I to have the Magic Circle drawn around me, too?" asked Cap'n Bill.

"Of course," answered Aquareine. "You will need no other protection than that, yet Princess Clia and I will both be with you. For to-day I shall leave Merla to rule our palaces in my place until we return."

No sooner was breakfast finished than Trot was anxious to start. The girl was also curious to discover what the powerful Magic Circle might prove to be, but she was a little disappointed in the ceremony. The queen merely grasped her fairy wand in her right hand and swam around the child in a circle, from left to right. Then she took her wand in her left hand and swam around Trot in another circle, from right to left.

"Now, my dear," said she, "you are safe from any creature we are liable to meet."

She performed the same ceremony for Cap'n Bill, who was doubtful about the Magic Circle, because he felt the same after it as he had before. But he said nothing of his unbelief, and soon they left the palace and started upon their journey.

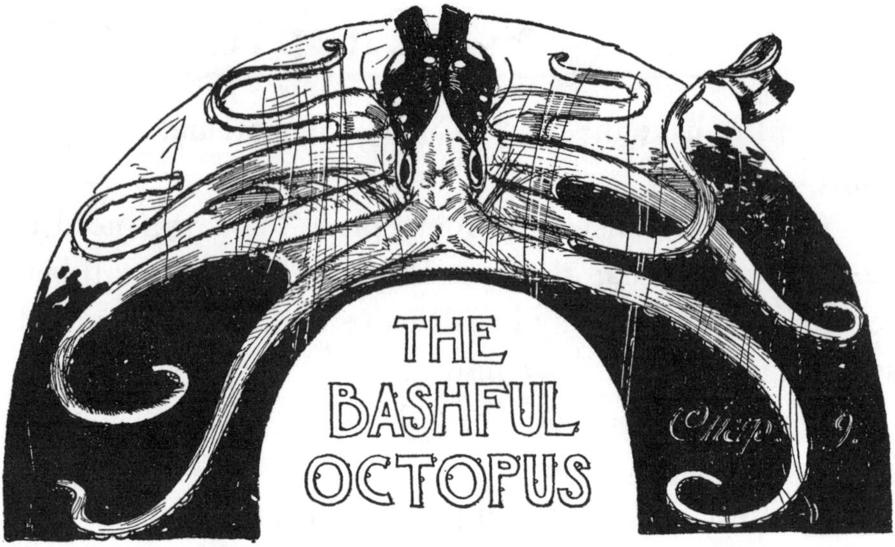
THE BASHFUL OCTOPUS
Chap. 9.

IT was a lovely day, and the sea was like azure under the rays of the sun.

Over the flower beds and through the gardens they swam, emerging into the open sea in a direction opposite that taken by the visitors the day before. The party consisted of but four: Queen Aquareine, Princess Clia, Trot and Cap'n Bill.

"People who live upon the land know only those sea creatures which they are able to catch in nets, or upon hooks, or those which become disabled and are washed ashore," remarked the Queen, as they swam swiftly through the clear water. "And those who sail in ships see only the creatures who chance to come to the surface. But, in the deep ocean caverns are queer beings, that no mortal has ever heard of or beheld, and some of these we are to visit. We shall also see some sea shrubs and flowering weeds, which are sure to delight you with their beauty."

The sights really began before they had gone very far from the palace, and a school of butterfly fish, having gorgeous colors spattered over their broad wings, was first to delight the strangers. They swam just as butterflies fly, with a darting, jerky motion, and called a merry "Good morning!" to the mermaids as they passed.

"These butterfly fish are remarkably active," said the Princess, "and their quick motions protect them from their enemies. We like to meet them; they are always so gay and good-natured."

"Why, so am I!" cried a sharp voice just beside them, and they all paused to discover what creature had spoken to them.

"Take care," said Clia, in a low voice. "It 's an octopus."

Trot looked eagerly around. A long, brown arm stretched across their way in front, and another just behind them; but that did not worry her. The octopus, himself, came slowly sliding up to them, and proved to be well worth looking at.

He wore a red coat with brass buttons, and a silk hat was tipped over one ear. His eyes were somewhat dull and watery and he had a moustache of long, hair-like "feelers" that curled stiffly at the ends. When he tried to smile at them he showed two rows of sharp, white teeth. In spite of his red coat and yellow embroidered vest, his standing collar and carefully tied cravat, the legs of the octopus were bare, and Trot noticed he used some of his legs for arms, as in one of them was held a slender cane, and in another, a handkerchief.

"Well, well!" said the Octopus. "Are you all dumb? Or don't you know enough to be civil when you meet a neighbor?"

"We know how to be civil to our friends," replied Trot, who did not like the way he spoke.

"Well, are n't we friends, then?" asked the Octopus, in an airy tone of voice.

"I think not," said the little girl. "Octopuses are horrid creatures."

"Octo*pi*, if you please; octo*pi*," said the monster, with a laugh.

"I don't see any pie that pleases me," replied Trot, beginning to get angry.

"Octo*pus* means one of us; two, or more are called octo*pi*," remarked the creature, as if correcting her speech.

"I suppose a lot of you would be a whole bakery!" she said, scornfully.

"Our name is latin. It was given us by learned scientists years ago," said the Octopus.

"That's true enough," agreed Cap'n Bill. "The learned scientists named ev'ry blamed thing they come acrost, an' gener'ly they picked out names as nobody could understand, or pernounce."

"That is n't our fault, sir," said the Octopus. "Indeed, it 's pretty hard for us to go through life with such terrible names. Think of the poor little sea horse. He used to be

a merry and cheerful fellow, but since they named him 'hippocampus' he has n't smiled once."

"Let 's go," said Trot; "I don't like to 'sociate with octopuses."

"Octo*pi*," said the creature, again correcting her.

"You 're jus' as horrid, whether you 're puses or pies," she declared.

"Horrid!" cried the monster, in a shocked tone of voice.

"Not only horrid, but horrible!" persisted the girl.

"May I ask in what way?" he inquired, and it was easy to see he was offended.

"Why, ev'rybody knows that octopuses are jus' wicked an' deceitful," she said. "Up on the earth, where I live, they call the Stannerd Oil Company an octopus, an' the Coal Trust an octopus, an'——"

"Stop, stop!" cried the monster, in a pleading voice. "Do you mean to tell me that the earth people, whom I have always respected, compare me to the Stannerd Oil Company?"

"Yes," said Trot, positively.

"That 's what they do," added Cap'n Bill, nodding his grizzled head.

"Oh, what a disgrace! What a deep, direful, dreadful disgrace!" moaned the Octopus, drooping his head in shame; and Trot could see great tears rolling down his cheeks.

"This comes of having a bad name," said the Queen, gently, for she was moved by the monster's grief.

"It is unjust! It is cruel and unjust!" sobbed the creature, mournfully. "Just because we have several long arms, and take whatever we can reach, they accuse us of being like—

like—oh, I cannot say it! It is too shameful—too humiliating!"

"Come; let's go," said Trot, again; so they left the poor octopus weeping and wiping his watery eyes with his handkerchief, and swam on their way.

"I'm not a bit sorry for him," remarked the child; "for his legs remind me of serpents."

"So they do me," agreed Cap'n Bill.

"But the octopi are not very bad," said the Princess, "and we get along with them much better than we do with their cousins the sea devils."

"Oh. Are the sea devils their cousins?" asked Trot.

"Yes; and they are the only creatures of the ocean which we greatly fear," replied Aquareine. "I hope we shall meet none to-day, for we are going near to the dismal caverns where they live."

"What are the sea devils like, ma'am?" inquired Cap'n Bill, a little uneasily.

"Something like the octopus you just saw, only much larger and of a bright scarlet color, striped with black," answered the Queen. "They are very fierce and terrible creatures, and nearly as much dreaded by the inhabitants of the ocean as is Zog, and nearly as powerful as King Anko himself."

The Sea Fairies

"Zog! Who is Zog?" questioned the girl. "I have n't heard of him, before now."

"We do not like to mention Zog's name," responded the Queen, in a low voice. "He is the wicked genius of the sea, and a magician of great power."

"What 's he like?" asked Cap'n Bill.

"He is a dreadful creature, part fish, part man, part beast and part serpent. Centuries ago they cast him off the earth into the sea, where he has caused much trouble. Once he waged a terrible war against King Anko, but the sea serpent finally conquered Zog, and drove the magician into his castle, where he now stays shut up. For if ever Anko catches the monster outside of his enchanted castle he will kill him, and Zog knows that very well."

"Seems like you have your troubles down here, just as we do on top the ground," remarked Cap'n Bill.

"But, I 'm glad old Zog is shut up in his castle," added Trot. "Is it a sea castle, like your own palaces?"

"I cannot say, my dear, for the enchantment makes it invisible to all eyes but those of its inhabitants," replied Aquareine. "No one sees Zog now, and we scarcely ever hear of him; but all the sea people know he is here, some place, and fear his power. Even in the old days, before Anko conquered him, Zog was the enemy of the mermaids, as he was of all the good and respectable seafolk. But do not worry

106

about the magician, I beg of you, for he has not dared to do an evil deed in many, many years."

"Oh, I'm not afraid," asserted Trot.

"I'm glad of that," said the Queen. "Keep together, friends, and be careful not to separate, for here comes an army of sawfishes."

Even as Aquareine spoke they saw a swirl and commotion in the water ahead of them, while a sound like a muffled roar fell upon their ears. Then swiftly there dashed upon them a group of great fishes, with long saws sticking out in front of their noses, armed with sharp hooked teeth, all set in a row. They were larger than the swordfishes and seemed more fierce and bold. But the mermaids and Trot, and Cap'n Bill quietly awaited their attack, and instead of tearing them with their saws, as they expected to do, the fishes were unable to touch them at all. They tried every possible way to get at their proposed victims, but the Magic Circle was all-powerful and turned aside the ugly saws; so our friends were not disturbed at all. Seeing this, the sawfishes soon abandoned the attempt and with growls and roars of disappointment swam away and were quickly out of sight.

Trot had been a wee bit frightened during the attack, but now she laughed gleefully and told the queen that it seemed very nice to be protected by fairy powers.

The water grew a darker blue as they descended into its

depths, farther and farther away from the rays of the sun. Trot was surprised to find she could see so plainly through the high wall of water above her; but the sun was able to shoot its beams straight down through the transparent sea, and they seemed to penetrate to every nook and crevice of the rocky bottom.

In this deeper part of the ocean some of the fishes had a phosphorescent light of their own, and these could be seen far ahead, as if they were lanterns. The explorers met a school of argonauts going up to the surface for a sail, and the child watched these strange creatures with much curiosity. The argonauts live in shells, in which they are able to hide in case of danger from prowling wolf fishes; but otherwise they crawl out and carry their shells like humps upon their backs. Then they spread their skinny sails above them and sail away under water till they come to the surface, where they float and let the currents of air carry them along the same as the currents of water had done before. Trot thought the argonauts comical little creatures, with their big eyes and sharp noses, and to her they looked like a fleet of tiny ships.

It is said that men got their first idea of boats, and of how to sail them, from watching these little argonauts.

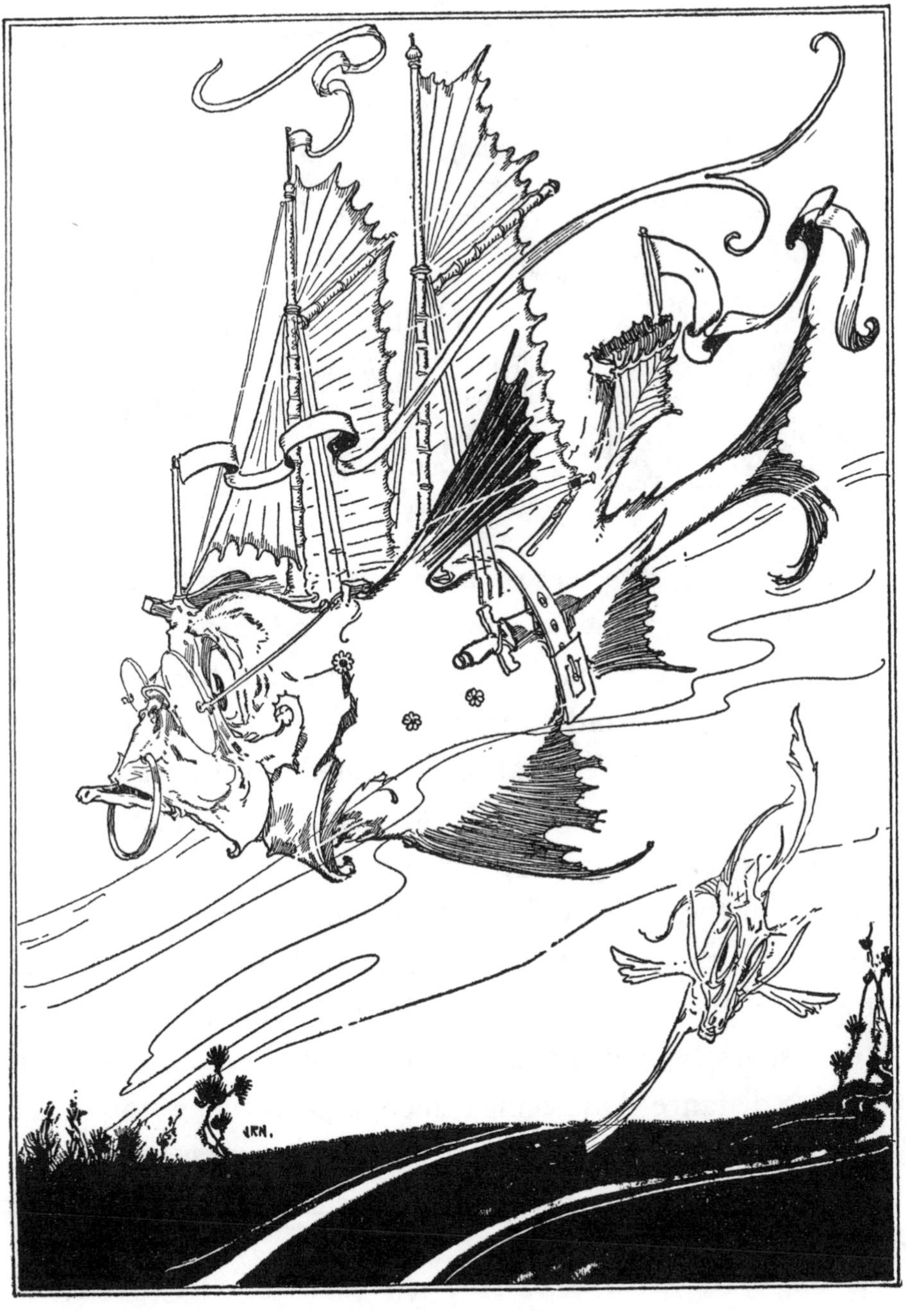
JRN.

THE
UNDISCOVERED
ISLAND

Chap. 10

IN following the fleet of argonauts the four explorers had
risen higher in the water and soon found they had wandered
to an open space that seemed to Trot like the flat top of a
high hill. The sands were covered with a growth of weeds
so gorgeously colored that one who had never peered beneath
the surface of the sea would scarcely believe they were not
the product of a dye shop. Every known hue seemed represented in the delicate fern-like leaves that swayed softly to
and fro as the current moved them. They were not set close
together, these branches of magnificent hues, but were scattered sparsely over the sandy bottom of the sea, so that while
from a distance they seemed thick, a nearer view found them
spread out with ample spaces of sand between them.

In these sandy spaces lay the real attractiveness of the

place, for here were many of those wonders of the deep that have surprised and interested people in all ages.

First were the starfishes—hundreds of them, it seemed— lying sleepily on the bottom, with their five or six points extended outward. They were of various colors, some rich and brilliant, others of dark brown hues. A few had wound their arms around the weeds, or were creeping slowly from one place to another, in the latter case turning their points downward and using them as legs. But most of them were lying motionless, and as Trot looked down upon them she thought they resembled stars in the sky on a bright night— except that the blue of the heavens was here replaced by the white sand, and the twinkling diamond stars by the colored starfish.

"We are near an island," said the Queen, "and that is why so many starfishes are here, as they love to keep close to shore. Also the little sea horses love these weeds and to me they are more interesting than the starfish."

Trot now noticed the sea horses for the first time. They were quite small—merely two or three inches high—but had funny little heads that were shaped much like the head of a horse, and bright, intelligent eyes. They had no legs, though, for their bodies ended in tails which they twined around the stems of seaweeds to support themselves, and keep the currents from carrying them away.

The Sea Fairies

Trot bent down close to examine one of the queer little creatures, and exclaimed: "Why, the sea horses have n't any fins, or anything to swim with."

"Oh, yes we have," replied the Sea Horse, in a tiny, but distinct voice. "These things on the side of my head are fins."

"I thought they were ears," said the girl.

"So they are. Fins and ears at the same time," answered the little sea animal. "Also, there are small fins on our backs. Of course, we can't swim as the mermaids do, or even as swiftly as fishes; but we manage to get around, thank you."

"Don't the fishes catch and eat you?" inquired Trot, curiously.

"Sometimes," admitted the Sea Horse, "and there are many other living things that have a way of destroying us. But here I am, as you see, over six weeks old, and during that time I have escaped every danger. That is n't so bad, is it?"

"Phoo!" said a Starfish lying near, "I 'm over three months old. You 're a mere baby, Sea Horse."

"I 'm not!" cried the Sea Horse, excitedly. "I 'm full-grown, and may live to be as old as you are!"

"Not if I keep on living," said the Starfish, calmly, and Trot knew he was correct in his statement.

The little girl now noticed several sea spiders creeping around, and drew back because she did not think them very pretty. They were shaped not unlike the starfishes, but had slender legs and big heads with wicked looking eyes sticking out of them.

"Oh, I don't like those things!" said Trot, coming closer to her companions.

"You don't, eh?" said a big Sea Spider, in a cross voice. "Why do you come around here, then, scaring away my dinner, when you're not wanted?"

"It isn't *your* ocean," replied Trot.

"No; and it isn't yours," snapped the Spider. "But as it's big enough for us both, I'd like you to go away."

"So we will," said Aquareine, gently, and at once she moved toward the surface of the water. Trot and Cap'n Bill followed, with Clia, and the child asked:

"What island are we near?"

"It has no name," answered the Queen, "for it is not inhabited by man, nor has it ever yet been discovered by them. Perhaps you will be the first humans to see this island. But it is a barren, rocky place, and only fit for seals and turtles."

"Are any of them there now?" Cap'n Bill inquired.

"I think so. We will see."

Trot was astonished to find how near they were to the "top" of the ocean, for they had not ascended through the water very long when suddenly her head popped into the air, and she gave a gasp of surprise to find herself looking at the clear sky for the first time since she had started upon this adventure, by rowing into Giant's Cave.

She floated comfortably in the water, with her head and face just out of it, and began to look around her. Cap'n Bill was at her side, and so were the two mermaids. The day was fair and the surface of the sea, which stretched far away as the eye could reach, rippled under a gentle breeze. They had risen almost at the edge of a small, rocky islet, high in the middle, but gradually slanting down to the water. No trees, or bushes, or grass grew anywhere about; only rocks, gray and bleak, were to be seen.

Trot scarcely noticed this at first, however, for the island seemed covered with groups of forms, some still and some moving, which the old sailor promptly recognized as seals. Many were lying asleep or sunning themselves; others crept awkwardly around, using their strong fins as legs or "paddles," and caring little if they disturbed the slumbers of the others. Once in a while, one of those crowded out of place would give a loud and angry bark, which awakened others and set them to barking likewise.

Baby seals were there in great numbers, and were more active and playful than their elders. It was really wonderful how they could scramble around on the land, and Trot laughed more than once at their antics.

Chapter Ten

At the edge of the water lay many huge turtles, some as big around as a wagon wheel and others much smaller in size.

"The big ones are very old," said the Queen, seeing Trot's eyes fixed on the turtles.

"How old?" asked the child.

"Hundreds of years, I think. They live to a great age, for nothing can harm them when they withdraw their legs and heads into their thick shells. We use some of the turtles for food, but prefer the younger ones. Men also fish for turtles and eat them, but, of course, no men ever come to this out-of-the-way place in the ocean, so the inhabitants of this little island know they are perfectly safe.'

In the center of the island rose high cliffs, on top of which were to be seen great flocks of sea-gulls, some whirling in the air, while others were perched upon the points of rock.

"What do the birds find to eat?" asked Cap'n Bill.

"They often feed upon seals which die of accident or old age, and they are expert fishermen," explained Queen Aquareine. "Curiously enough, the seals also feed upon these birds, which they are often able to catch in their strong jaws, when the gulls venture too near. And then, the seals frequently rob the nests of eggs, of which they are very fond."

I'd like a few gulls' eggs now," remarked a big seal that lay near them upon the shore. Trot had thought him sound asleep, but now he opened his eyes to blink lazily at the group in the water.

"Good morning," said the Queen. "Are n't you Chief Muffruff?"

"I am," answered the old seal. "And you are Aquareine, the mermaid queen. You see I remember you, although you have n't been here for years. And is n't that Princess Clia? To be sure! But the other mermaids are strangers to me; especially the bald-headed one."

"I 'm not a mermaid," asserted Cap'n Bill. "I 'm a sailor, jes' a-visitin' the mermaids."

"Our friends are earth dwellers," explained the Queen.

"That 's odd," said Muffruff. "I can't remember that any earth dwellers ever came this way before. I never travel far, you see, for I 'm chief of this disorderly family of seals that live on this island—on it and off it, that is."

"You 're a poor chief," said a big turtle lying beside the seal. "If your people are disorderly it is your own fault."

Muffruff gave a chuckling laugh. Then, with a movement quick as lightning, he pushed his head under the shell of the turtle and gave it a sudden jerk. The huge turtle was tossed up on edge and then turned flat on its back, where its short legs struggled vainly to right its overturned body.

"There!" snorted the Seal, contemptuously. "Perhaps

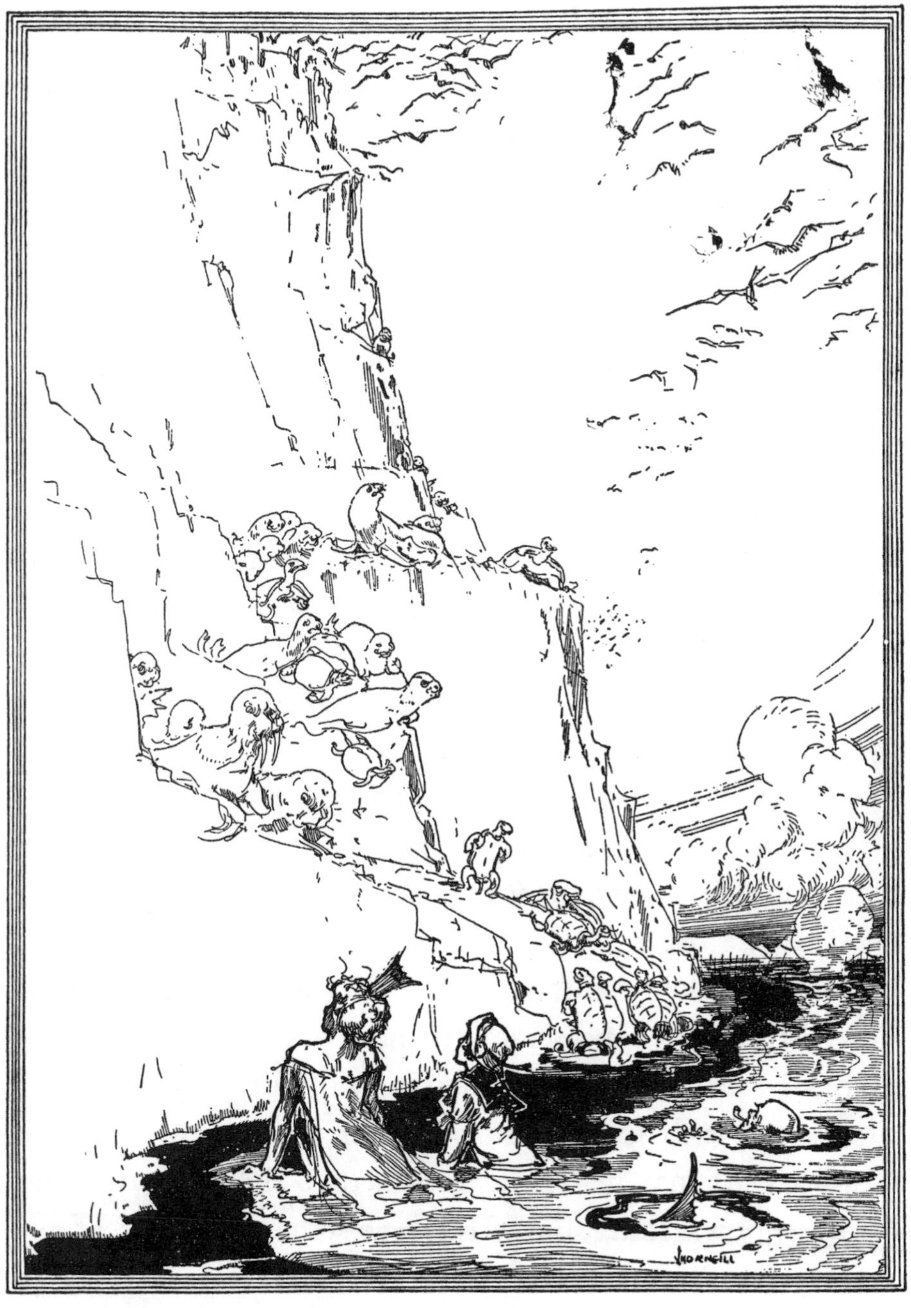

you'll dare insult me again in the presence of visitors, you old mud-wallower!"

Seeing the plight of the turtle, several young seals came laughingly wabbling to the spot, and as they approached the helpless creature drew in his legs and head, and closed his two shells tightly together. The seals bumped against the turtle and gave it a push that sent it sliding down the beach like a toboggan, and a minute later it splashed into the water and sank out of sight.

But that was just what the creature wanted. On shore the upset turtle was quite helpless; but the mischievous seals saved him. For as soon as he touched the water he was able to turn and right himself, which he promptly did. Then he raised his head above the water and asked:

"Is it peace, or war, Muffruff?"

"Whichever you like," answered the Seal, indifferently.

Perhaps the turtle was angry, for it ran on shore with remarkable swiftness, uttering a shrill cry as it advanced. At once all the other turtles awoke to life, and with upraised heads joined their comrade in the rush for the seals. Most of Chief Muffruff's band scrambled hastily down the rocks and plunged into the water of the sea, without waiting for the turtles to reach them; but the chief himself was slow in escaping. It may be he was ashamed to run while the mermaids were watching, but if this was so he made a great mistake. The turtles snapped at his fins and tail, and began biting round chunks out of them, so that Chief Muffruff screamed with pain and anger, and floundered into the water as fast as he could go. The vengeful turtles were certainly the victors, and now held undisputed possession of the island.

Trot laughed joyously at the incident, not feeling a bit sorry for the old seal who had foolishly begun the battle. Even the gentle queen smiled as she said:

"These quarrels between the turtles and seals are very frequent, but they are soon ended. An hour from now they will all be lying asleep together, just as we found them; but we will not wait for that. Let us go."

She sank slowly beneath the water again, and the others followed after her.

ZOG THE TERRIBLE AND HIS SEA DEVILS
Chap. 11.

"THE sun must be going under a cloud," said Trot, looking ahead.

They had descended far into the ocean depths again—further, the girl thought, than they had ever been before.

"No," the Queen answered, after a glance ahead of them; "that is a cuttlefish, and he is dyeing the sea around him with ink, so that he can hide from us. Let us turn a little to the left, for we could see nothing at all in that inky water."

Following her advice they made a broad curve to the left, and at once the water began to darken in that direction, too.

"Why, there's another of 'em," said Cap'n Bill, as the little party came to a sudden halt.

"So there is," returned the Queen, and Trot thought there was a little quiver of anxiety in her voice. "We must go far to the right to escape the ink."

Chapter Eleven

So they again started, this time almost at a right angle to their former course, and the little girl inquired:

"How can the cuttlefish color the water so very black?"

"They carry big sacks in front of them, where they conceal the ink," Princess Clia answered. "Whenever they choose, the cuttlefish are able to press out this ink, and it colors the water for a great space around them."

The direction in which they were now swimming was taking them far out of their way. Aquareine did not wish to travel very far to the right, so, when she thought they had gone far enough to escape the inky water, she turned to lead her party toward the left—the direction in which she *did* wish to go. At once, another cloud of ink stained the water, and drove them to the right again.

"Is anything wrong, ma'am?" asked Cap'n Bill, seeing a frown gather upon the queen's lovely face.

"I hope not," she said. "But I must warn you that these cuttlefish are the servants of the terrible sea devils, and from the way they are acting they seem determined to drive us toward the Devil Caves, which I wished to avoid."

This admission on the part of their powerful protector, the fairy mermaid, sent a chill to the hearts of the earth people. Neither spoke for a time, but finally Cap'n Bill asked in a timid voice:

"Had n't we better go back, ma'am?"

"Yes," decided Aquareine, after a moment's thought. "I think it will be wise to retreat. The sea devils are evidently aware of our movements and wish to annoy us. For my part I have no fear of them. but I do not care to have you meet such creatures."

But when they turned around to abandon their journey another inky cloud was to be seen behind them. They really had no choice but to swim in the only streak of clear water they could find, and the mermaids well knew this would lead them nearer and nearer to the caves of their enemies.

But Aquareine led the way, moving very slowly, and the others followed her. In every other direction they were hemmed in by the black waters, and they did not dare to halt, because the inky fluid crept swiftly up behind them and drove them on.

The queen and the princess had now become silent and grave. They swam on either side of their guests, as if to better protect them.

"Don't look up," whispered Clia, pressing close to the little girl's side

"Why not?" asked Trot; and then she did exactly what she had been told not to do. She lifted her head and saw stretched over them a network of scrawny crimson arms, interlaced like the branches of trees in winter, when the leaves have fallen and left them bare.

Chapter Eleven

Cap'n Bill gave a start and muttered "Land sakes!" for he, too, had gazed upward and seen the crimson network of limbs.

"Are these the sea devils?" asked the child, more curious than frightened.

"Yes, dear," replied the Queen. "But I advise you to pay no attention to them. Remember, they cannot touch us."

In order to avoid the threatening arms overhead, which followed them as they swam, our friends kept near to the bottom of the sea, which was here thickly covered with rough and jagged rocks. The inky water had now been left far behind, but, when Trot looked over her shoulder, she shuddered to find a great crimson monster following closely after them, with a dozen long, snaky feelers stretched out as if to grab anyone that lagged behind. And there, at the side of Princess Clia, was another sea devil, leering silently with his cruel, bulging eyes at the pretty mermaid. Beside the queen swam still another of their enemies. Indeed, the sea devils had crept upon them and surrounded them everywhere except at the front, and Trot began to feel nervous and worried for the first time.

Cap'n Bill kept mumbling queer words under his breath, for he had a way of talking to himself when anything "upsot him," as he would quaintly remark. Trot always knew he was disturbed or in trouble when he began to "growl."

The Sea Fairies

The only way now open was straight ahead. They swam slowly, yet fast enough to keep a safe distance from the dreadful creature behind them.

"I'm afraid they are driving us into a trap," whispered the Queen, softly; "but, whatever happens, do not lose courage, earth friends. Clia and I are here to protect you, and our fairy powers are sufficient to keep you from all harm."

"Oh, I don't mind so very much," declared Trot, calmly. "It's like the fairy adventures in storybooks, and I've often thought I'd like that kind of adventures, 'cause the story always turns out the right way."

Cap'n Bill growled something just then, but the only words Trot could make out were, "never lived to tell the tale."

"Oh, pshaw, Cap'n," she said; "we may be in danger, right enough, an' to be honest I don't like the looks of these sea devils at all. But, I'm sure it's no *killing* matter, for we've got the fairy circles all around us."

"Ha, ha!" laughed the monster beside her. "*We* know all about the fairy circles, don't we, Migg?"

"Ho, ho!" laughed the monster on the other side; "we do, Slibb, my boy; and we don't think much of fairy circles, either!"

"They have foiled our enemies many a time," declared the Princess, with much dignity.

124

"Ha, ha!" laughed one; "that's why we're here now."

"Ho, ho!" laughed the other; "we've learned a trick or two, and we've got you fast this time."

Then all the sea devils—those above and the one behind, and the two on the sides—laughed all together, and their laughter was so horrible that it made even Trot shudder.

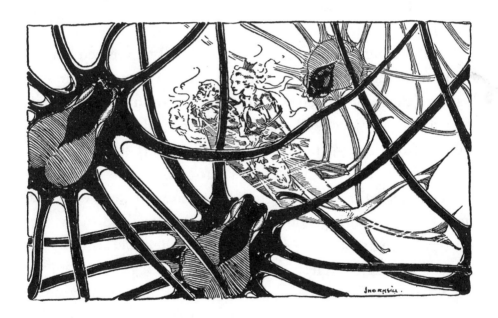

But, now the queen stopped short, and the others stopped with her.

"I will go no farther," she said, firmly, not caring if the creatures overheard her. "It is evident that these monsters are trying to drive us into some secret place, and it is well-known that they are in league with Zog the Terrible, whom they serve because they are as wicked as he is. We must be somewhere near the hidden castle of Zog, so I prefer to stay here rather than be driven into some place far more dangerous. As for the sea devils, they are powerless to injure us in any way. Not one of the thousand arms about us can possibly touch our bodies."

The only reply to this defiant speech was another burst of horrible laughter; and now there suddenly appeared before them still another of the monsters, which thus completely hemmed them in. Then the creatures began interlacing their long arms—or "feelers"—until they formed a perfect cage around the prisoners, not an opening being left that was large enough for one of them to escape through.

The mermaids and the girl and sailorman kept huddled close together, for, although they might be walled in by the sea devils, their captors could not touch them because of the protecting magic circles.

All at once Trot exclaimed: "Why, we must be moving!"

This was startling news, but by watching the flow of the water past them they saw that the little girl was right. The sea devils were swimming, all together, and as the cage they were in moved forward our friends were carried with it.

Queen Aquareine had a stern look upon her beautiful face. Cap'n Bill guessed from this look that the mermaid was angry, for it seemed much like the look Trot's mother wore when they came home late to dinner. But however angry the queen might be, she was unable to help herself or her guests just now, or to escape from the guidance of the dreaded sea devils. The rest of the party had become sober and thoughtful, and in dignified silence they awaited the outcome of this strange adventure.

THE ENCHANTED ISLAND

Chap 12

ALL at once it grew dark around them. Neither Cap'n Bill nor Trot liked this gloom, for it made them nervous not to be able to see their enemies.

"We must be near a sea cavern, if not within one," whispered Princess Clia, and even as she spoke the network of scarlet arms parted before them, leaving an avenue for them to swim out of the cage. There was brighter water ahead, too, so the queen said, without hesitation:

"Come along, dear friends; but, let us clasp hands and keep close together."

They obeyed her commands and swam swiftly out of their prison and into the clear water before them, glad to put a distance between themselves and the loathesome sea devils. The monsters made no attempt to follow them, but they burst into a chorus of harsh laughter which warned our friends that they had not yet accomplished their escape.

The four now found themselves in a broad, rocky passage, which was dimly lighted from some unknown source. The walls overhead, below them and at the sides all glistened, as if made of silver, and in places were set small statues of birds, beasts and fishes, occupying niches in the walls and seemingly made from the same glistening material.

The queen swam more slowly, now that the sea devils had been left behind, and she looked exceedingly grave and thoughtful.

"Have you ever been here before?" asked Trot.

"No, dear," said the Queen, with a sigh.

"And do you know where we are?" continued the girl.

"I can guess," replied Aquareine. "There is only one place in all the sea where such a passage as that we are in could exist without my knowledge, and that is in the hidden dominions of Zog. If we are indeed in the power of that fearful magician we must summon all our courage to resist him, or we are lost!"

"Is Zog more powerful than the mermaids?" asked Trot, anxiously.

"I do not know, for we have never before met to measure our strength," answered Aquareine. "But if King Anko could defeat the magician, as he surely did, then I think I shall be able to do so."

"I wish I was sure of it," muttered Cap'n Bill.

Absolute silence reigned in the silver passage. No fish were there; not even a sea flower grew to relieve the stern grandeur of this vast corridor. Trot began to be impressed with the fact that she was a good way from her home and mother, and she wondered if she would ever get back again to the white cottage on the cliff. Here she was, at the bottom of the great ocean, swimming through a big tunnel that had an enchanted castle at one end, and a group of horrible sea devils at the other! In spite of this thought she was not very much afraid. Although two fairy mermaids were her companions, she relied, strange to say, more upon her tried and true friend Cap'n Bill, than upon her newer acquaintances to see her safely out of her present troubles.

Cap'n Bill himself did not feel very confident.

"I don't care two cents what becomes o' me," he told Princess Clia, in a low voice, "but I'm drea'ful worried over our Trot. She's too sweet an' too young to be made an end of in this 'ere fashion."

Clia smiled at the speech.

"I'm sure you will find the little girl's end a good way off," she replied. "Trust to our powerful queen, and be sure she will find some means for us all to escape uninjured."

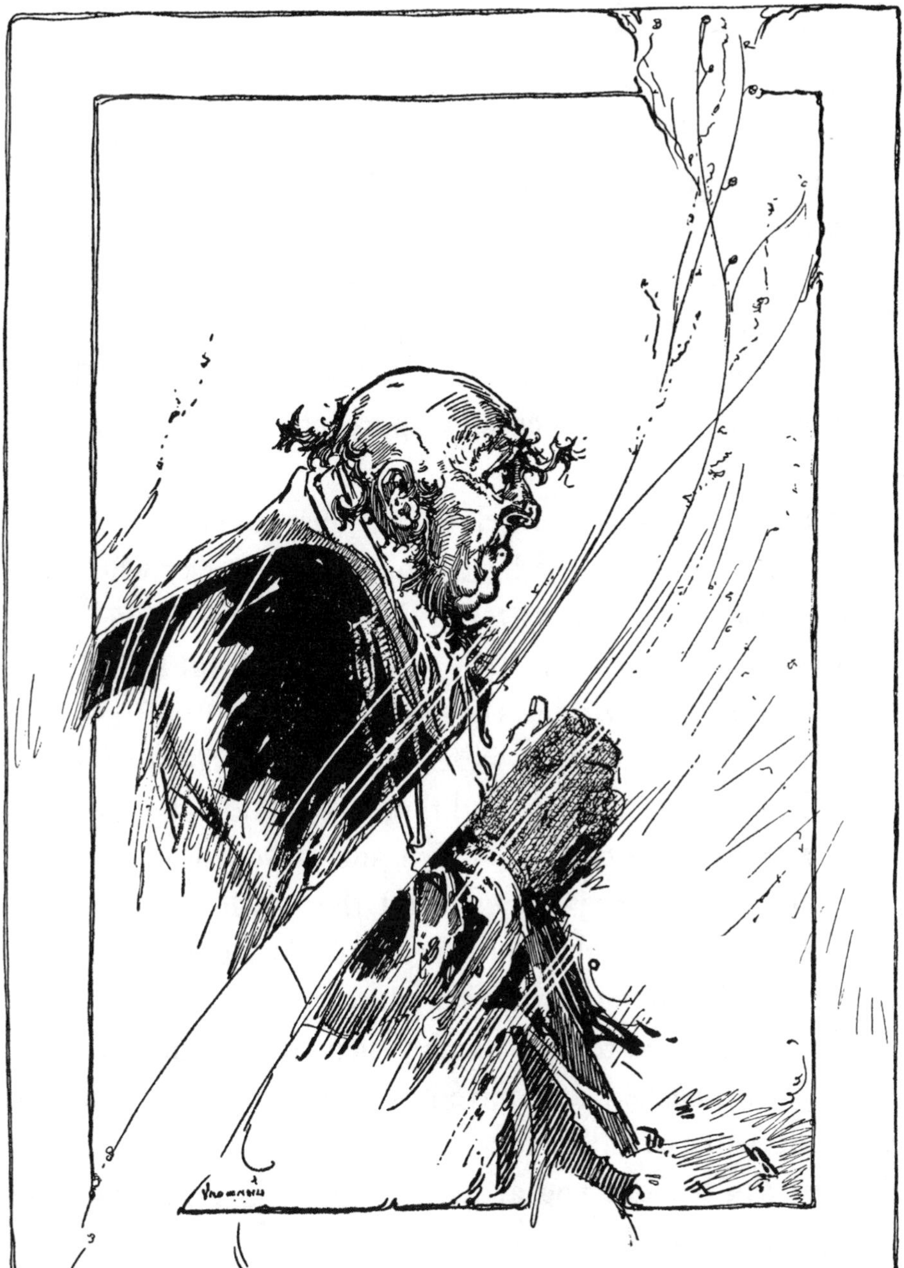

The Sea Fairies

The light grew brighter as they advanced, until finally they perceived a magnificent archway just ahead of them. Aquareine hesitated a moment whether to go on, or turn back; but there was no escaping the sea devils behind them, and she decided the best way out of their difficulties was to bravely face the unknown Zog, and rely upon her fairy powers to prevent his doing any mischief to herself or her friends. So she led the way, and together they approached the archway and passed through it.

They now found themselves in a vast cavern, so great in extent that the dome overhead looked like the sky when seen from the earth. In the center of this immense sea cavern rose the towers of a splendid castle, all built of coral inlaid with silver, and having windows of clear glass.

Surrounding the castle were beds of beautiful sea flowers, many being in full bloom, and these were laid out with great care in artistic designs. Goldfish and silverfish darted here and there among the foliage, and the whole scene was so pretty and peaceful that Trot began to doubt there was any danger lurking in such a lovely place.

As they paused to look around them, a brilliantly colored gregfish approached and gazed at them curiously with his big, saucer-like eyes.

"So Zog has got you at last!" he said in a pitying tone.

Chapter Twelve

"How foolish you were to swim into that part of the sea where he is powerful."

"The sea devils made us," explained Clia.

"Well, I 'm sorry for you, I 'm sure," remarked the Greg, and with a flash of his tail he disappeared among the sea foliage.

"Let us go to the castle," said the Queen, in a determined voice. "We may as well boldly defy our fate as to wait until Zog seeks us out."

So they swam to the entrance of the castle. The doors stood wide open and the interior seemed as well lighted as the cavern itself, although none of them could discover from whence the light came.

At each side of the entrance lay a fish such as they had never seen before. It was flat as a doormat, and seemed to cling fast to the coral floor. Upon its back were quills, like those of a porcupine, all pointed and sharp. From the center of the fish arose a head shaped like a round ball, with a circle of piercing, bead-like eyes set in it. These strange guardians of the entrance might be able to talk and to tell what their numerous eyes saw, yet they remained silent and watchful. Even Aquareine gazed upon them curiously, and she gave a little shudder as she did so.

Inside the entrance was a domed hall, with a flight of stairs leading to an upper balcony. Around the hall were several doorways hung with curtains made of woven sea-weeds. Chairs and benches stood against the wall, and these astonished the visitors because neither stairs nor chairs seemed useful in a kingdom where every living thing was supposed to swim and have a fish's tail. In Queen Aquareine's palaces benches for reclining were used, and stairs were wholly un-necessary; but in the Palace of Zog the furniture and fittings were much like those of a house upon earth, and, except that every space was here filled with water instead of air, Trot and Cap'n Bill might have imagined themselves in a hand-some earthly castle.

The little group paused half fearfully in the hall, yet so far, there was surely nothing to be afraid of. They were wondering what to do next, when the curtains of an archway were pushed aside and a boy entered. To Trot's astonishment he had legs, and walked upon them naturally and with per-fect ease. He was a delicate, frail looking little fellow, dressed in a black velvet suit with knee breeches. The bows at his throat and knees were of colored seaweeds, woven into broad ribbons. His hair was yellow, and banged across his forehead. His eyes were large and dark, with a pleasant, merry sparkle in them. Around his neck he wore a high ruff, but in spite of this Trot could see that below his plump cheeks were several scarlet-edged slits that looked like the gills of fishes, for they gently opened and closed as the boy breathed in the water by which he was surrounded. These gills did not greatly mar the lad's delicate beauty, and he spread out his arms and bowed low and gracefully in greeting.

"Hello," said Trot.

"Why, I'd like to," replied the boy, with a laugh, "but, being a mere slave, it is n't proper for me to hello. But it's good to see earth people again, and I'm glad you're here."

"We're not glad," observed the girl; "we're afraid."

"You'll get over that," declared the boy, smilingly. "People lose a lot of time being afraid. Once I was myself afraid, but I found it was no fun, so I gave it up."

"Why were we brought here?" inquired Queen Aquareine, gently.

"I can't say, madam, being a mere slave," replied the boy. "But, you have reminded me of my errand. I am sent to inform you all that Zog the Forsaken, who hates all the world and is hated by all the world, commands your presence in his den."

"Do you hate Zog, too?" asked Trot.

"Oh, no," answered the boy. "People lose a lot of time in hating others, and there's no fun in it at all. Zog may be hateful, but I'm not going to waste time hating him. You may do so, if you like."

"You are a queer child," remarked the Mermaid Queen, looking at him attentively. "Will you tell us who you are?"

"Once, I was Prince Sacho of Sacharhineolaland, which is a sweet country, but hard to pronounce," he answered. "But in this domain I have but one title and one name, and that is 'Slave.'"

"How came you to be Zog's slave?" asked Clia.

"The funniest adventure you ever heard of," asserted the boy, with eager pride. "I sailed in a ship that went to pieces in a storm. All on board were drowned but me—and I came mighty near it, to tell the truth. I went down deep, deep into the sea, and at the bottom was Zog, watching the people drown. I tumbled on his head and he grabbed and saved me, saying I would make a useful slave. By his magic power he made me able to live under water, as the fishes live, and he brought me to this castle and taught me to wait upon him, as his other slaves do."

"Is n't it a dreadful, lonely life?" asked Trot.

"No, indeed," said Sacho; "we have n't any time to be lonely, and the dreadful things Zog does are very exciting and amusing, I assure you. He keeps us guessing every minute, and that makes the life here interesting. Things were getting a bit slow an hour ago, but now that you are here I 'm in hopes we will all be kept busy and amused for some time."

"Are there many others in the castle besides you and Zog?" asked Aquareine.

"Dozens of us. Perhaps hundreds. I 've never counted

Chapter Twelve

them," said the boy. "But Zog is the only master; all the rest of us are in the same class, so there is no jealousy among the slaves."

"What is Zog like?" Cap'n Bill questioned.

At this the boy laughed, and the laugh was full of mischief.

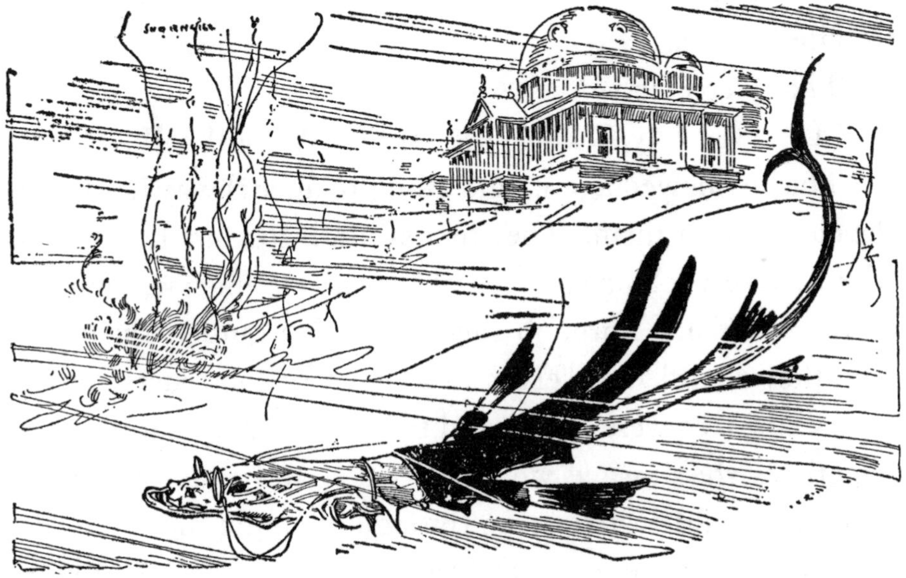

"If I could tell you what Zog is like it would take me a year," was the reply. "But I can't tell you. Every one has a different idea of what he 's like, and soon you will see him yourselves."

"Are you fond of him?" asked Trot.

"If I said yes, I 'd get a good whipping," declared Sacho.

"I am commanded to hate Zog, and being a good servant I try to obey. If anyone dared to like Zog I am sure he 'd be instantly fed to the turtles; so I advise you not to like him."

"Oh, we won't," promised Trot.

"But we 're keeping the master waiting, and that is also a dangerous thing to do," continued the boy. "If we don't hurry up Zog will begin to smile, and when he smiles there is trouble brewing."

The queen sighed.

"Lead the way, Sacho," she said. "We will follow."

The boy bowed again, and going to an archway held aside the curtains for them. They first swam into a small anteroom which led into a long corridor, at the end of which was another curtained arch. Through this Sacho also guided them, and now they found themselves in a cleverly constructed maze. Every few feet were twists and turns, and sharp corners, and sometimes the passage would be wide, and again so narrow that they could just squeeze through in single file.

"Seems like we 're gettin' further into the trap," growled Cap'n Bill. "We could n't find our way out o' here to save our lives."

"Oh, yes we could," replied Clia, who was just behind him. "Such a maze may indeed puzzle you, but the queen or I could lead you safely through it again, I assure you. Zog is not so clever as he thinks himself."

Chapter Twelve

The sailor, however, found the maze very bewildering, and so did Trot. Passages ran in every direction, crossing and recrossing, and it seemed wonderful that the boy Sacho knew just which way to go. But he never hesitated an instant. Trot looked carefully to see if there were any marks to guide him, but every wall was of plain, polished marble, and every turning looked just like all the others.

Suddenly Sacho stopped short. They were now in a broader passage, but as they gathered around their conductor, they found further advance blocked. Solid walls faced them, and here the corridor seemed to end.

"Enter!" cried a clear voice.

"But we can't!" protested Trot.

"Swim straight ahead," whispered the boy, in soft tones. "There is no real barrier before you. Your eyes are merely deceived by magic."

"Ah, I understand," said Aquareine, nodding her pretty head. And then she took Mayre's hand and swam boldly forward, while Cap'n Bill followed holding the hand of Clia. And behold! the marble wall melted away before them, and they found themselves in a chamber more splendid than even the fairy mermaids had ever seen before.

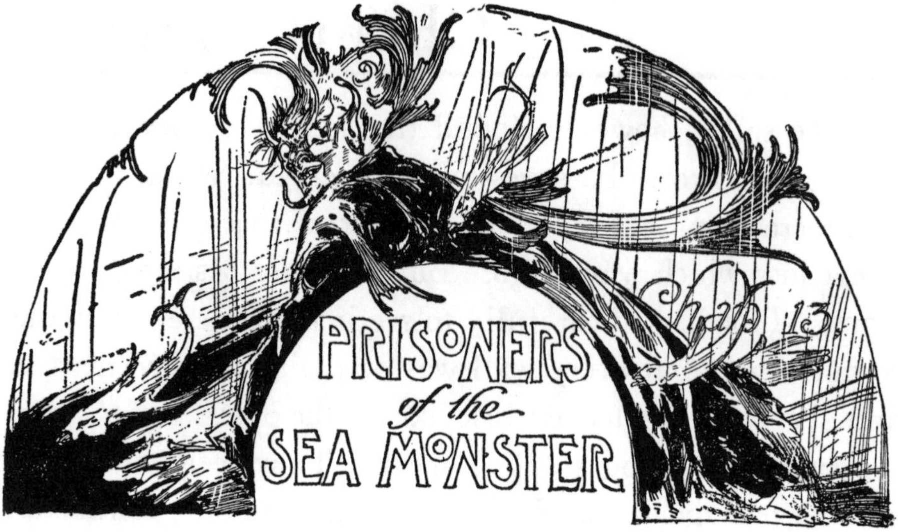
Chap. 13.
PRISONERS
of the
SEA MONSTER

THE room in the enchanted castle which Zog called his "den," and in which the wicked sea monster passed most of his time, was a perfectly shaped dome of solid gold. The upper part of this dome was thickly set with precious jewels—diamonds, rubies, sapphires and emeralds, which sparkled beautifully through the crystal water. The lower walls were as thickly studded with pearls, all being of perfect shape and color. Many of the pearls were larger than any which may be found upon earth, for the sea people know where to find the very best, and hide them away where men cannot discover them.

The golden floor was engraved with designs of rare beauty, depicting not only sea life, but many adventures upon land. In the room were several large golden cabinets, the doors of which were closed and locked, and in addition to the cabinets there were tables, chairs and sofas, the latter upholstered with softest sealskins. Handsome rugs of exquisitely woven seaweeds were scattered about, the colors of which were artistically blended together. In one corner a fountain of air bubbled up through the water.

The entire room was lighted as brilliantly as if exposed to the direct rays of the sun, yet where this light came from our friends could not imagine. No lamp or other similar device was visible anywhere.

The strangers at first scarcely glanced at all these beautiful things, for in an easy chair sat Zog himself, more wonderful than any other living creature, and as they gazed upon him their eyes seemed fascinated, as if held by a spell.

Zog's face was the face of a man, except that the tops of his ears were pointed like horns and he had small horns instead of eyebrows, and a horn on the end of his chin. In spite of these deformities the expression of the face was not unpleasant, or repulsive. His hair was carefully parted and brushed, and his mouth and nose were not only perfect in shape, but quite handsome.

Only the eyes betrayed Zog and made him terrible to all beholders. They seemed like coals of glowing fire, and sparkled so fiercely that no one ever cared to meet their gaze for more than an instant. Perhaps the monster realized this, for he usually drooped his long lashes over his fiery eyes to shut out their glare.

Zog had two well shaped legs which ended in the hoofs of beasts, instead of feet, and these hoofs were shod with gold. His body was a shapeless mass covered with richly embroidered raiment, over which a great robe of cloth of gold fell in many folds. This robe was intended to hide the magician's body from view, but Trot noticed that the cloth moved constantly, in little ripples, as if what lay underneath would not keep still.

The best features of which Zog could boast were his arms and hands, the latter being as well formed, as delicate and white as those of a well-bred woman. When he spoke, his voice sounded sweet and clear, and its tones were very gentle. He had given them a few moments to stare at him, for he was examining them, in turn, with considerable curiosity.

"Well," said he, "do you not find me the most hateful creature you have ever beheld?"

The queen refrained from answering, but Trot said, promptly:

"We do. Nothing could be more horrider or more disgustin' than you are, it seems to me."

"Very good; very good, indeed," declared the monster, lifting his lashes to flash his glowing eyes upon her. Then

Chapter Thirteen

he turned toward Cap'n Bill. "Man-fish," he continued, "what do *you* think of me?"

"Mighty little," the sailor replied. "You orter be 'shamed to ask sech a question, knowin' you look worse ner the devil himself."

"Very true," answered Zog, frowning. He felt that he had received a high compliment, and the frown showed he was pleased with Cap'n Bill.

But now Queen Aquareine advanced to a position in front of their captor and said:

"Tell me, Zog; why have you trapped us and brought us here?"

"To destroy you," was the quick answer, and the magician turned for an instant to flash his eyes upon the beautiful mermaid. "For two hundred years I have been awaiting a chance to get within my power some friend of Anko the Sea Serpent—of Anko, whom I hate!" he added, smiling sweetly. "When you left your palace to-day my swift spies warned me, and so I sent the sea devils to capture you. Often have they tried to do this before, but always failed. To-day, acting by my command, they tricked you, and by surrounding you, forced you to the entrance of my enchanted castle. The result is a fine capture of important personages. I have now in my power the queen and princess of the fairy mermaids, as well as two wandering earth people, and I assure you I shall take great enjoyment in destroying you utterly."

"You are a coward," declared the Queen, proudly. "You dared not meet us in the open sea."

"No; I dare not leave this castle," Zog admitted, still smiling. "But here, in my own domain, my power is supreme. Nothing can interfere with my vengeance."

"That remains to be seen," said Aquareine, firmly meeting the gaze of the terrible eyes.

"Of course," he answered, nodding his head with a graceful movement. "You will try to thwart me and escape. You will pit your fairy power against my powers of magic. This will give me great pleasure, for the more you struggle the greater will be my revenge."

"But why should you seek revenge upon us?" asked Clia. "We have never harmed you."

"That is true," replied Zog. "I bear you no personal ill will. But you are friends of my great enemy, King Anko, and it will annoy him very much when he finds that you have been destroyed by me. I cannot hurt the rascally old sea serpent himself, but through you I can make him feel my vengeance."

"The mermaids have existed thousands of years," said the Queen, in a tone of pride. "Do you imagine the despised and conquered Zog has power to destroy them?"

Chapter Thirteen

"I do not know," was the quiet answer. "It will be interesting to discover which is the more powerful."

"I challenge you to begin the test at once, vile magician!" exclaimed Aquareine.

"There is no hurry, fair Queen," answered Zog, in his softest tones. "I have been so many years in accomplishing your capture that it is foolish to act hastily now. Besides, I am lonely. Here, in my forced retirement, I see only those uninteresting earth mortals whom I have made my slaves, for all sea dwellers are forbidden to serve me save the sea devils, and they dare not enter my castle. I have saved many mortals from drowning and brought them here to people my castle, but I do not love mortals. Two lovely mermaids are much more interesting, and before I allow you to perish I shall have much amusement in witnessing your despair, and your struggles to escape. You are now my prisoners. By slow degrees I shall wear out your fairy powers and break your hearts, as well as the hearts of these earth dwellers who have no magic powers, and I think it will be a long time before I finally permit you to die."

"That's all right," said Trot, cheerfully. "The longer I live the better I'll be satisfied."

"That's how I feel about it," added Cap'n Bill. "I on't get in a hurry to kill us, Zog; it'll be such a wear an' tear on your nerves. Jes' take it easy an' let us live as long as we can."

"Don't you care to die?" asked the magician.

"It's a thing I never longed for," the sailor replied. "You see, we had no business to go on a trip with the mermaids, to begin with. I've allus heard tell that mermaids is dangerous, an' no one as met 'em ever lived to tell the tale. Eh, Trot?"

"That's what you said, Cap'n Bill."

"So, I guess we're done for, one way 'r 'nother; an' it don't matter much which. But Trot's a good child, an' mighty young an' tender. It don't seem like her time has come to die. I'd like to have her sent safe home to her mother. So I've got this 'ere propersition to make, Zog: If your magic could make *me* die twice, or even *three* times fer good measure, why you go ahead an' do it an' I won't complain. All I ask is fer you to send this little girl safe back to dry land again."

"Don't you do it, Zog!" cried Trot, indignantly, and turning to Cap'n Bill she added: "I'm not goin' to leave you down here in all this mess, Cap'n, and don't you think it. If one of us gets out of the muddle we're in, we'll both get out; so don't you make any bargains with Zog to die twice."

Zog listened to this conversation very carefully.

"The dying does not amount to much," he said; "it is the

thinking about it that hurts you mortals most. I 've watched many a shipwreck at sea, and the people would howl and scream for hours before the ship broke up. Their terror was very enjoyable. But when the end came they all drowned as peacefully as if they were going to sleep, so it did n't amuse me at all."

"I 'm not worrying," said Trot.

"Ner me," said Cap'n Bill. "You 'll find we can take what comes jes' as easy as anybody."

"I do not expect to get much fun from you poor mortals," said Zog, carelessly. "You are merely a side show to my circus—a sort of dessert to my feast of vengeance. When the time comes I can find a hundred ways to kill you. My most interesting prisoners are these pretty mermaids, who claim that none of their race has ever yet died, or been destroyed. The first mermaid ever created is living yet—and I am told she is none other than Queen Aquareine. So I have a pretty problem before me, to invent some way to destroy the mermaids, or put them out of existence. And it will require some thought."

"Also, it will require some power you do not possess," suggested the Queen.

"That may be," replied Zog, softly; "but I am going to experiment, and I believe I shall be able to cause you a lot of pain and sorrow before I finally make an end of you. I have not lived twenty-seven thousand years, Aquareine, without getting a certain amount of wisdom, and I am more powerful than you suspect."

"You are a monster and a wicked magician," said the Mermaid Queen.

"I am," agreed Zog; "but I cannot help it. I was created part man, part bird, part fish, part beast and part reptile, and such a monstrosity could not be otherwise than wicked. Everybody hates me, and I hate everybody."

"Why don't you kill yourself?" asked Trot.

"I've tried that, and failed," he answered. "Only one being in the world has power to destroy me, and that is King Anko, the sea serpent."

"Then you'd better let him do it," advised the little girl.

"No; much as I long to die, I cannot allow King Anko the pleasure of killing me. He has always been my worst enemy, and it would be such a joy to him to kill me that I really cannot allow him. Indeed, I have always hoped to kill Anko. I have now been three thousand six hundred and forty-two years, eleven months and nine days figuring out a plan to destroy old Anko, and as yet I have not discovered a way."

"I'd give it up, if I were you," advised Trot. "Don't you think you could get some fun out of trying to be good?"

"No!" cried Zog, and his voice was not so soft as before. "Listen, Aquareine: You and your attendants shall be prisoners in this castle until I can manage to stop you from living. Rooms will be placed at your disposal, and I wish you to go to them at once, as I am tired of looking at you."

"You're no more tired than we are," remarked Trot. "It's lucky you can't see yourself, Zog."

He turned his glowing eyes full upon her.

"The worst of my queer body I keep concealed," he said. "If ever you see it, you will scream with terror."

He touched a bell beside him and the girl was surprised to find how clearly its tones rang out through the water. In an instant the boy Sacho appeared and bowed low before his dreadful master.

"Take the mermaids and the child to the Rose Chamber," commanded Zog; "and take the old man-fish to the Peony Room."

Sacho turned to obey.

"Are the outer passages well guarded?" asked the monster.

"Yes; as you have commanded," said the boy.

"Then you may allow the prisoners to roam at will throughout the castle. Now, go!"

The prisoners followed Sacho from the room, glad to get away. The presence of this evil being had grown oppressive to them, and Zog had himself seemed ill at ease during the last few minutes. The robe so closely wound around his body moved jerkily, as if something beneath disturbed it, and at such times Zog shifted nervously in his seat.

Sacho's thin little legs trotted through the water, and led the way into a different passage from the one by which they had entered. They swam slowly after him and breathed easier when they had left the golden domed chamber, where their wicked enemy sat enthroned.

"Well, how do you like him?" asked Sacho, with a laugh.

"We hate him!" declared Trot, emphatically.

"Of course you do," replied Sacho. "But, you 're wasting time hating anything. It does n't do you any good, or him any harm. Can you sing?"

"A little," said Trot; "but I don't feel like singing now."

"You 're wrong about that," the boy asserted. "Anything that keeps you from singing is foolishness, unless it 's

laughter. Laughter, joy and song are the only good things in the world."

Trot did not answer this queer speech, for just then they came to a flight of stairs, and Sacho climbed up them, while the others swam. And now they were in a lofty, broad corridor having many doors hung with seaweed draperies. At one of these doorways Sacho stopped and said:

"Here is the Rose Chamber, where the master commands you to live until you die. You may wander anywhere in the castle as you please; to leave it is impossible. Whenever you return to the Rose Chamber you will know it by this design of roses, sewn in pearls upon the hangings. The Peony Room, where the man-fish is to live, is the next one farther on."

"Thank you," replied Queen Aquareine. "Are we to be fed?"

"Meals will be served in your rooms. If you desire anything, ring the bell and some of the slaves will be sure to answer it. I am mostly in attendance upon my master, but whenever I am at liberty I will look after your comfort myself."

Again they thanked the strange boy, and he turned and left them. They could hear him whistle and sing as he returned along the passage. Then Princess Clia parted the curtains that her queen and companions might enter the Rose Chamber.

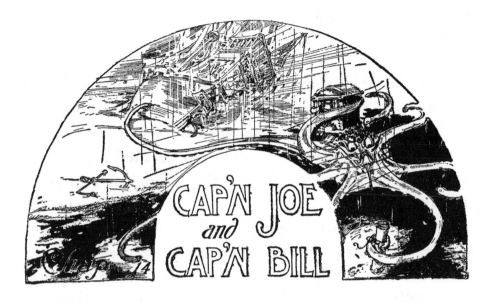

CAP'N JOE
and CAP'N BILL

THE rooms Zog had given his prisoners were as handsome as all other parts of this strange, enchanted castle. Gold was used plentifully in the decorations, and in the Rose Chamber occupied by the mermaids and Trot, golden roses formed a border around the entire room. The sea maidens had evidently been expected, for the magician had provided couches for them to recline upon, similar to the ones used in the mermaid palaces. The frames were of mother-of-pearl and the cushions of soft, white sponges. In the room were toilet tables, mirrors, ornaments and many articles used by earth people, which they afterward learned had been plundered by Zog from sunken ships and brought to his castle by his allies, the sea devils.

While the mermaids were examining and admiring their room, Cap'n Bill went to the Peony Room to see what it was like, and found his quarters very cosy and interesting. There were pictures on the walls—portraits of grave-looking porpoises, bashful seals, and smug and smiling walruses. Some of the wall panels were formed of mirrors and reflected clearly the interior of the room. Around the ceiling was a frieze of imitation peonies in silver, and the furniture was peony-shaped, the broad leaves being bent to form seats and couches.

Beside a pretty dressing table hung a bell cord, with a tassel at the end. Cap'n Bill did not know it was a bell cord, so he pulled it to see what would happen and was puzzled to find that nothing seemed to happen at all, the bell being too far away for him to hear it. Then he began looking at the treasures contained in this royal apartment, and was much pleased with a golden statue of a mermaid, that resembled Princess Clia in feature. A silver flower vase upon a stand contained a bouquet of gorgeous peonies, "as nat'ral as life," said Cap'n Bill, although he saw plainly that they must be made of metal.

Trot came in just then to see how her dear friend was located. She entered from the doorway that connected the two rooms, and said:

"Isn't it pretty, Cap'n? And who'd ever think that awful creature Zog owned such a splendid castle, and kept his prisoners in such lovely rooms?"

"I once heard tell," said the sailor, "of a foreign people

that sacrificed human bein's to please their pagan gods; an' before they killed 'em outright they stuffed the victims full o' good things to eat, an' dressed 'em in pretty clothes, an' treated 'em like princes. That's why I don't take much comfort in our fine surroundin's, Trot. This Zog is a pagan, if ever there was one, an' he don't mean us any good, you may depend on 't."

"No," replied Trot, soberly; "I'm sure he does n't expect us to be happy here. But, I'm going to fool him and have just as good a time as I can."

As she spoke they both turned around—an easy thing to do with a single flop of their flexible tails—and Cap'n Bill uttered a cry of surprise. Just across the room stood a perfect duplicate of himself. The round head, with its bald top and scraggly whiskers, the sailor cap and shirt, the wide pantaloons—even the wooden leg—each and every one were exact copies of those owned by Cap'n Bill. Even the expression in the light blue eyes was the same, and it is no wonder the old sailor stared at his "double" in amazement. But the next minute he laughed, and said:

"Why, Trot, it's *me* reflected in a mirror. But, at first, I thought it was some one else."

Trot was staring, too.

"Look, Cap'n!" she whispered; "look at the wooden leg."

"Well, it's *my* wooden leg, ain't it?" he inquired.

"If it is, it can't be a reflection in a mirror," she argued, "for *you* have n't got a wooden leg. You 've got a fish's tail."

The old sailor was so startled by this truth that he gave a great flop with his tail that upset his balance, and made him keel a somersault in the water before he got right side up again. Then he found the other sailorman laughing at him, and was horrified to find the "reflection" advancing toward them, by stumping along on its wooden leg.

"Keep away! Git out, there!" yelled Cap'n Bill. "You 're a ghost—the ghost o' me that once was—an' I can't bear the sight o' you. Git out!"

"Did you ring jes' to tell me to git out?" asked the other, in a mild voice.

"I—I didn't ring," declared Cap'n Bill.

"You did; you pulled that bell cord," said the one-legged

"Oh; did pullin' that thing ring a bell?" inquired the Cap'n, a little ashamed of his ignorance and reassured by hearing the "ghost" talk.

"It surely did," was the reply; "and Sacho told me to answer your bell an' look after you. So I 'm a-lookin' after you."

"I wish you would n't," protested Cap'n Bill. "I 've no use fer—fer—ghostses, anyhow."

The strange sailor began to chuckle at hearing this, and

his chuckle was just like Cap'n Bill's chuckle—so full of merry humor that it usually made every one laugh with him.

"Who are you?" asked Trot, who was very curious and much surprised.

"I'm Cap'n Joe," was the reply. "Cap'n Joe Weedles, formerly o' the brig 'Gladsome' an' now a slave o' Zog at the bottom o' the sea."

"J—J—Joe Wee—Weedles!" gasped Cap'n Bill, amazed; "Joe Weedles o' the 'Gladsome'! Why, dash my eyes, mate, you must be my brother!"

"Are *you* Bill Weedles?" asked the other. And then he added: "But, no; you can't be. Bill was n't no merman. He were a human critter, like myself."

"That's what *I* am," said Cap'n Bill, hastily; "I'm a human critter, too. I've jes' borrered this fishtail to swim with while I'm visitin' the mermaids."

"Well, well," said Cap'n Joe, in astonishment; "who'd 'a' thought it! An' who'd ever 'a' thought as I'd find my long lost brother in Zog's enchanted castle, full fifty fathoms deep down in the wet, wet water!"

"Why, as fer that," replied Cap'n Bill, "it's *you* as is the long lost brother, not me. You an' your ship disappeared many a year ago, an' ain't never been heard of since; while, as fer me, I'm livin' on earth yet."

"You don't look it, to all appearances," remarked Cap'n

Joe, in a reflective tone of voice. "But I 'll agree it 's many a year since I saw the top o' the water, an' I 'm not expectin' to ever tramp on dry land again."

"Are you dead, or drownded, or what?" asked Cap'n Bill.

"Neither one nor t'other," was the answer. "But Zog gave me gills, so 's I could live in the water like fishes do, an' if I got on land I could n't breathe air any more 'n a fish out o' water can. So I guess as long as I live I 'll hev to stay down here."

"Do you like it?" asked Trot.

"Oh, I don't objec' much," said Cap'n Joe. "There ain't much excitement here, fer we don't catch a flock o' mermaids ev'ry day; but the work is easy an' the rations fair. I might 'a' been worse off, you know, for when my brig was wrecked I 'd 'a' gone to Davy Jones's Locker if Zog had n't happened to find me an' made me a fish."

"You don't look as much like a fish as Cap'n Bill does," observed Trot.

"P'raps not," said Cap'n Joe; "but I notice Bill ain't got any gills, an' breathes like you an' the mermaids does. When he gets back to land he 'll have his two legs again, an' live in comfort breathin' air."

"I won't have two legs," asserted Cap'n Bill, "for when I 'm on earth I 'm fitted with one wooden leg, jes' the same as you are, Joe."

"Oh; I had n't heard o' that, Bill; but I 'm not surprised," replied Brother Joe. "Many a sailor gets to wear a wooden leg, in time. Mine 's hick'ry."

"So 's mine," said Cap'n Bill, with an air of pride. "I 'm glad I 've run across you, Joe, for I often wondered what had become of you. Seems too bad, though, to have you spend all your life under water."

"What 's the odds?" asked Cap'n Joe. "I never could keep away from the water since I was a boy, an' there 's more dangers to be met floatin' on it than there is soakin' in it. An' one other thing pleases me when I think on it: I 'm parted from my wife—a mighty good woman with a tongue like a two-edge sword—an' my pore widder 'll get the insurance money an' live happy. As fer me, Bill, I 'm a good deal happier than I was when she kep' scoldin' me from mornin' to night every minute I was home."

"Is Zog a kind master?" asked Trot.

"I can't say he 's kind," replied Cap'n Joe, "for he 's as near a devil as any livin' critter *can* be. He grumbles an' growls in his soft voice all day, an' hates himself an' everybody else. But I don't see much of him. There 's so many of us slaves here that Zog don't pay much attention to us, an' we have a pretty good time when the ol' magician is shut up in his den, as he mostly is."

"Could you help us to escape?" asked the child.

"Why, I don't know how," admitted Cap'n Joe. "There's magic all around us, and we slaves are never allowed to leave this great cave. I'll do what I can, o' course; but Sacho is the boy to help you, if anyone can. That little chap knows a heap, I can tell you. So now, if nothin' more's wanted, I must get back to work."

"What work do you do?" Cap'n Bill asked.

"I sew buttons on Zog's clothes. Every time he gets mad he busts his buttons off, an' I have to sew 'em on again. As he's mad most o' the time, it keeps me busy."

"I'll see you again, won't I, Joe?" said Cap'n Bill.

"No reason why you should n't—if you manage to keep alive," said Cap'n Joe. "But you must n't forget, Bill, that Zog has his grip on you, an' I've never known anything to escape him yet."

Saying this the old sailor began to stump toward the door, but tripped his foot against his wooden leg and gave a swift dive forward. He would have fallen flat had he not grabbed the drapery at the doorway, and saved himself by holding fast to it with both hands. Even then he rolled and twisted so awkwardly before he could get upon his legs that Trot had to laugh outright at his antics.

"This hick'ry leg," said Cap'n Joe, "is so blamed light that it always wants to float. Agga-Groo, the goldworker, has promised me a gold leg, that will stay down; but he never

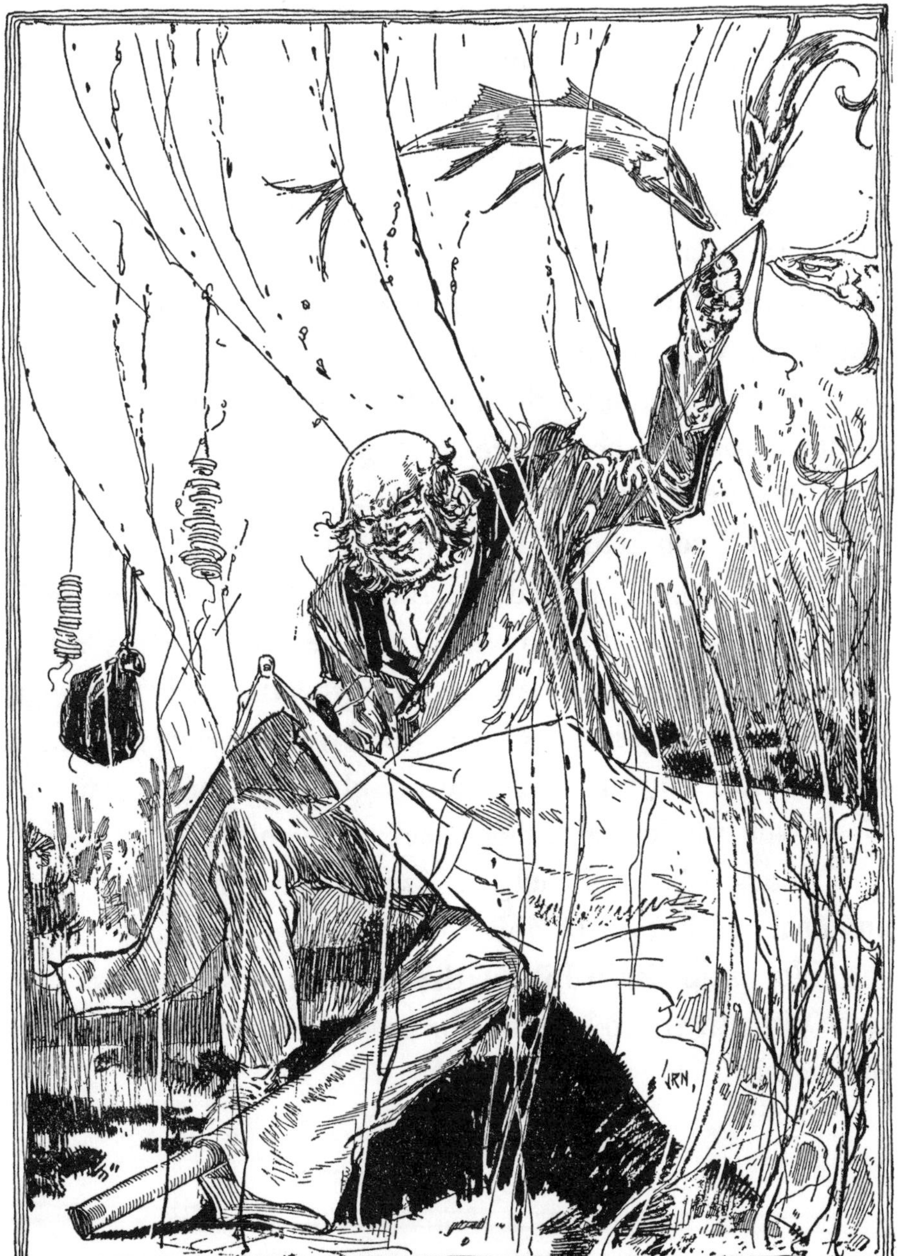

has time to make it. You're mighty lucky, Bill, to have a merman's tail, instead o' legs."

"I guess I am, Joe," replied Bill; "for in such a wet country the fishes have the best of it. But I ain't sure I'd like this sort o' thing always."

"Think o' the money you'd make in a side show," said Cap'n Joe, with his funny chuckling laugh. Then he pounded his wooden leg against the hard floor, and managed to hobble from the room without more accidents.

When he had gone, Trot said:

"Are n't you glad to find your brother again, Cap'n Bill?"

"Why, so-so," replied the sailor. "I don't know much about Joe, seein' as we have n't met before for many a long year; an' all I remember about our boyhood days is that we fit an' pulled hair most o' the time. But what worries me most is Joe's lookin' so much like me myself—wooden leg an' all. Don't you think it's rather cheeky an' unbrotherly, Trot?"

"Perhaps he can't help it," suggested the child. "And, anyhow, he'll never be able to live on land again."

"No," said Cap'n Bill, with a sigh, "Joe's a fish, now, an' so he ain't likely to be took for me by any of our friends on the earth."

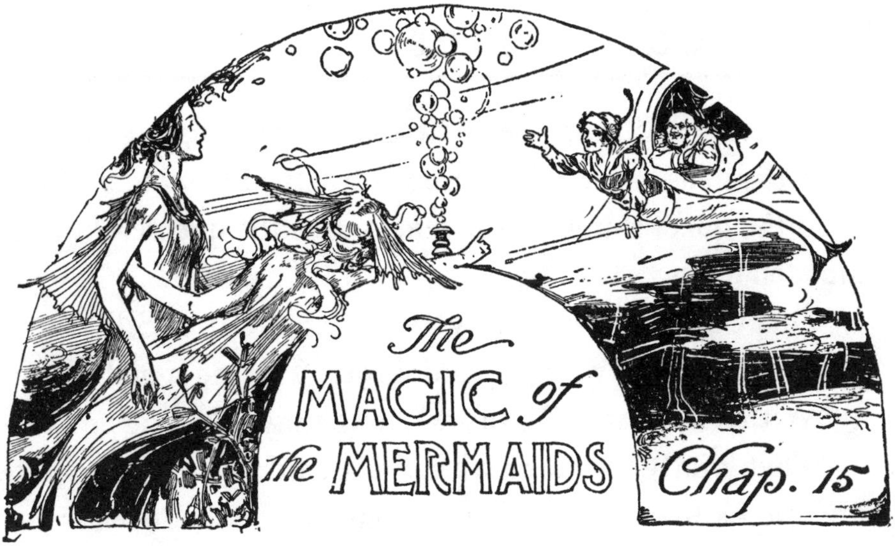
The MAGIC of the MERMAIDS
Chap. 15

WHEN Trot and Cap'n Bill entered the Rose Chamber they found the two mermaids reclining before an air fountain that was sending thousands of tiny bubbles up through the water.

"These fountains of air are excellent things," remarked Queen Aquareine, "for they keep the water fresh and sweet, and that is the more necessary where it is confined by walls, as it is in this castle. But, now let us counsel together, and decide what to do in the emergency that confronts us."

"How can we tell what to do, without knowing what 's going to happen?" asked Trot.

"Something 's sure to happen," said Cap'n Bill.

As if to prove his words a gong suddenly sounded at their door, and in walked a fat little man clothed all in white, including a white apron and white cap. His face was round and jolly, and he had a big mustache that curled up at the ends.

"Well, well!" said the little man, spreading out his legs and putting his hands on his hips as he stood looking at them; "of all the queer things in the sea, you 're the queerest! Mermaids, eh?"

"Don't bunch us that way!" protested Cap'n Bill.

"You are quite wrong," said Trot; "I 'm a—a girl."

"With a fish's tail?" he asked, laughing at her.

"That 's only just for a while," she said; "while I 'm in the water, you know. When I 'm at home on the land I walk just as you do—an' so does Cap'n Bill."

"But we have n't any gills," remarked the Cap'n, looking closely at the little man's throat; "so I take it we 're not as fishy as some others."

"If you mean me, I must admit you are right," said the little man, twisting his mustaches. "I 'm as near a fish as a man can be. But you see, Cap'n, without the gills that make me a fish I could not live under water."

"When it comes to that, you 've no business to live under water," asserted the sailor. "But I s'pose you 're a slave and can't help it."

"I 'm chief cook for that old horror, Zog. And that reminds me, good mermaids—or good people, or good girls and sailors, or whatever you are—that I 'm sent here to ask what you 'd like to eat."

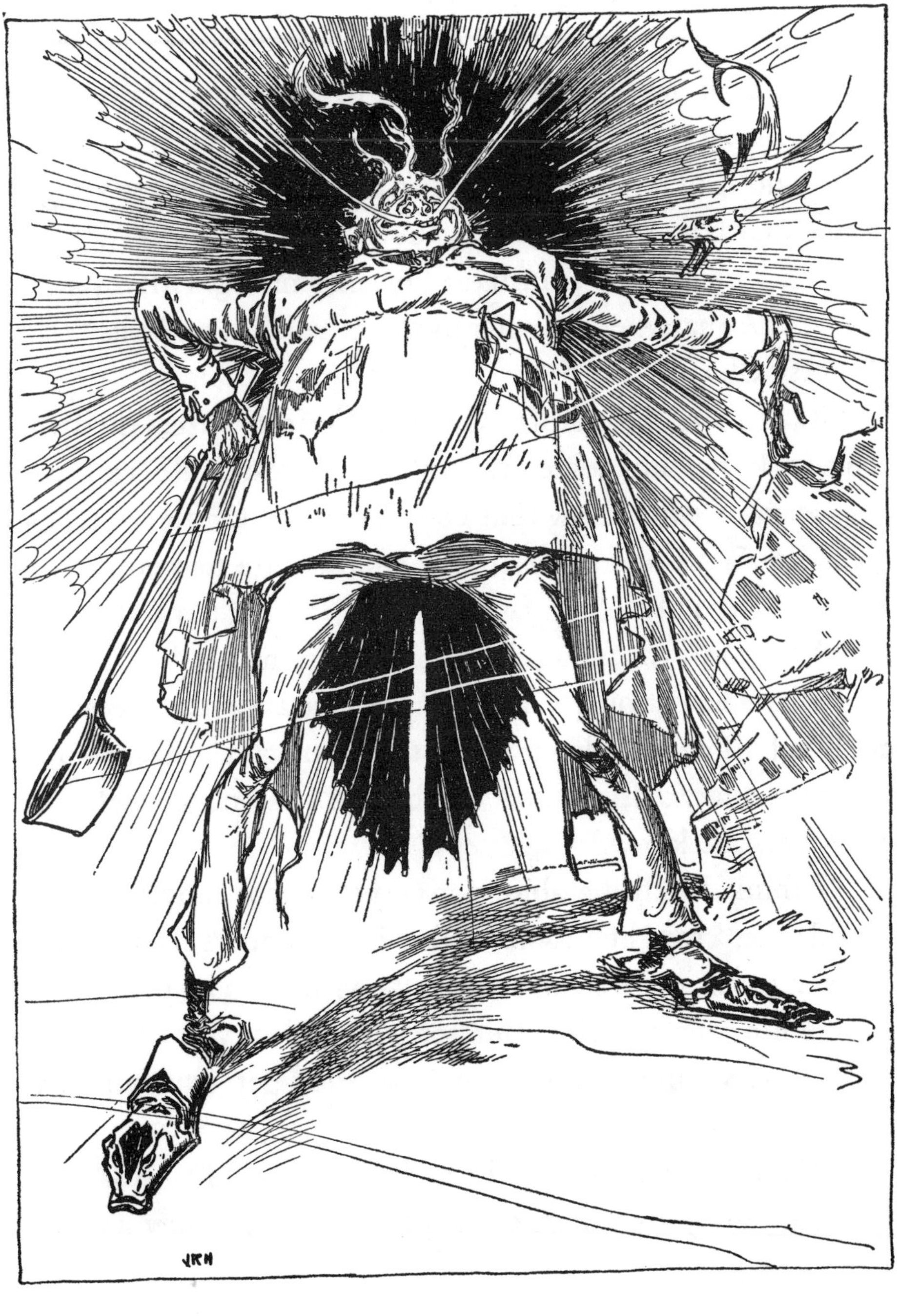

"Glad to see you, sir," said Cap'n Bill. "I'm nearly starved, myself."

"I had it in mind," said the little man, "to prepare a regular mermaid dinner; but since you're not mermaids—"

"Oh, two of us are," said the Queen, smiling. "I, my good cook, am Aquareine, the ruler of the mermaids, and this is the Princess Clia."

"I've often heard of you, your Majesty," returned the chief cook, bowing respectfully, "and I must say I've heard only good of you. Now that you have unfortunately become my master's prisoners it will give me pleasure to serve you as well as I am able."

"We thank you, good sir," said Aquareine.

"What have you got to eat?" inquired Trot. "Seems to me I'm hollow way down to my toes—my tail, I mean—and it'll take a lot to fill me up. We haven't eaten a morsel since breakfast, you know."

"I think I shall be able to give you almost anything you would like," said the cook. "Zog is a wonderful magician, and can procure anything that exists with no more effort than a wiggle of his thumb. But some eatables, you know, are hard to serve under water, because they get so damp that they are soon ruined."

"Ah, it is different with the mermaids," said Princess Clia.

"Yes; all your things are kept dry because they are surrounded by air. I've heard how the mermaids live. But here it is different."

"Take this ring," said the Queen, handing the chief cook a circlet which she drew from her finger. "While it is in your possession the food you prepare will not get wet—or even moist."

"I thank your Majesty," returned the cook, taking the ring. "My name is Tom Atto, and I'll do my best to please you. How would you like for luncheon some oysters on the half shell, clam broth, shrimp salad, broiled turtle steak and watermelon?"

"That will do very nicely," answered the Queen.

'Do watermelons grow in the sea?" asked Trot.

"Of course; that is why they are called watermelons," replied Tom Atto. "I think I shall serve you a water ice, in addition to the rest. Water ice is an appropriate sea food."

"Have some water cress with the salad," said Cap'n Bill.

"I'd thought of that," declared the cook. "Does n't my bill of fare make your mouths water?"

"Hurry up and get it ready," suggested Trot.

Tom Atto at once bowed and retired, and when they were alone, Cap'n Bill said to the queen:

"Do you think, ma'am, we can manage to escape from Zog and his castle?"

"I hope we shall find a way," replied Aquareine. "The

evil powers of magic, which Zog controls, may not prove to be as strong as the fairy powers I possess; but of course I cannot be positive until I discover what this wicked magician is able to do."

Princess Clia was looking out of one of the windows.

"I think I can see an opening far up in the top of the dome," she said.

They all hastened to the windows to look, and although Trot and Cap'n Bill could see nothing but a solid dome above the castle—perhaps, because it was so far away from them—the sharp eyes of Aquareine were not to be deceived.

"Yes," she announced, "there is surely an opening in the center of the great dome. A little thought must convince us that such an opening is bound to exist, for otherwise the water confined within the dome would not be fresh or clear."

"Then, if we could escape from this castle, we could swim up to the hole in the dome and get free!" exclaimed Trot.

"Why, Zog has probably ordered the opening well guarded, as he has all other outlets," responded the Queen. "Yet it may be worth while for us to make the attempt to get back into the broad ocean this way. The night would be the best time, when all are asleep; and surely it will be quicker to reach the ocean through this hole in the roof, than by means of the long, winding passages by which we entered."

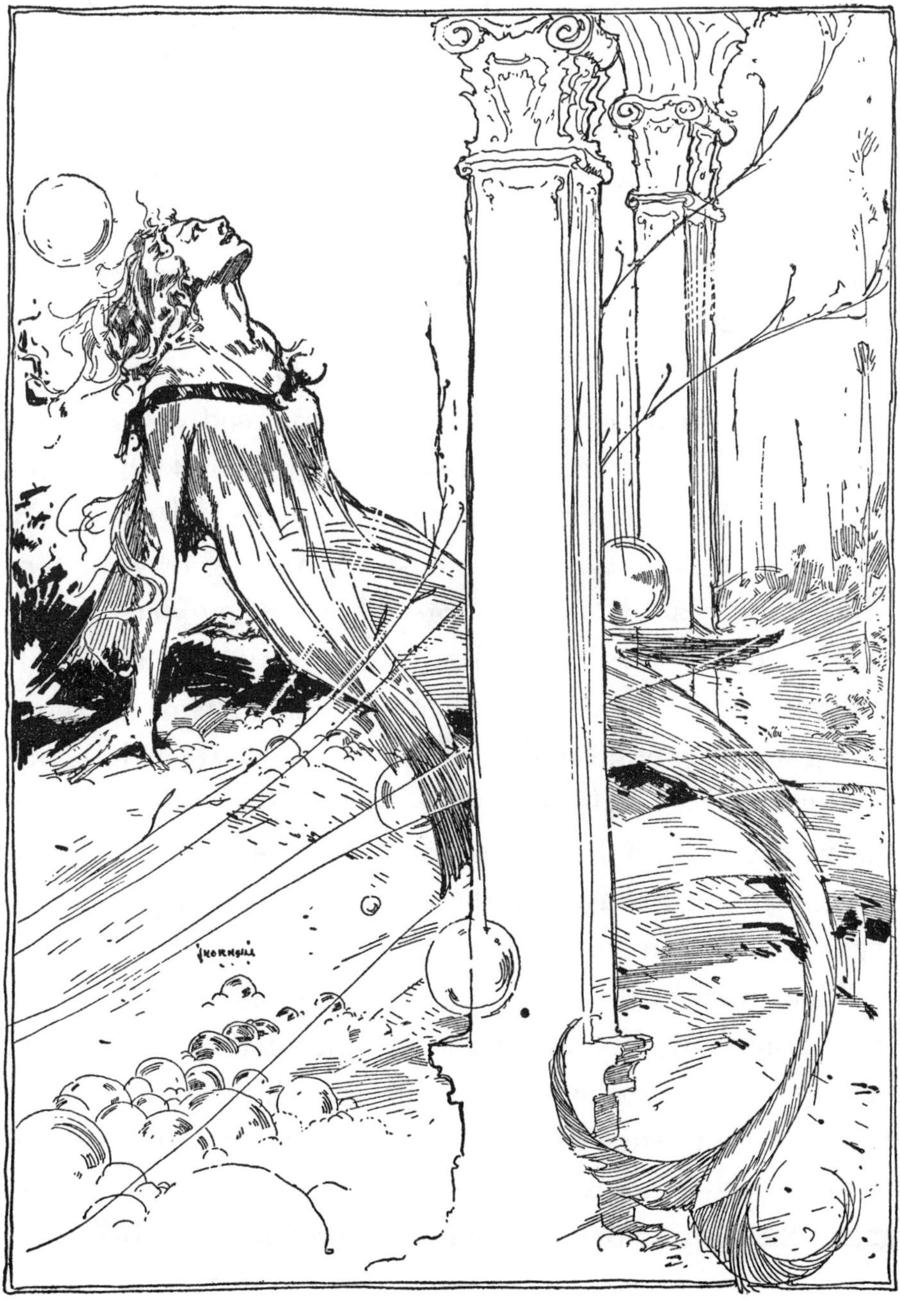

"But we will have to break out of the castle, in some way," observed Cap'n Bill.

"That will not be difficult," answered Aquareine. "It will be no trouble for me to shatter one of these panes of glass, allowing us to pass out and swim straight up to the top of the dome."

"Let's do it now!" said Trot, eagerly.

"No, my dear; we must wait for a good opportunity, when we are not watched closely. We do not wish the terrible Zog to thwart our plan," answered the Queen, gently.

Presently, two sailor boys entered, bearing trays of food which they placed upon a large table. They were cheery-faced young fellows, with gills at their throats but had laughing eyes, and Trot was astonished not to find any of the slaves of Zog weeping or miserable. Instead, they were as jolly and good-natured as could be, and seemed to like their life under the water. Cap'n Bill asked one of these boys how many slaves were in the castle, and the youth replied that he would try to count them and let him know.

Tom Atto had, they found, prepared for them an excellent meal, and they ate heartily because they were really hungry. After luncheon Cap'n Bill smoked his pipe contentedly and they renewed their conversation, planning various ways to outwit Zog and make their escape. While thus engaged the gong at the door sounded and Sacho entered.

Chapter Fifteen

"My diabolical master commands you to attend him," said the boy.

"When?" asked Aquareine.

"At once, your Majesty."

"Very well; we will follow you," she said.

So they swam down the corridors, following Sacho, until they again reached the golden domed room they had formerly visited.

Here sat Zog, just as they had left him, seemingly; but when his prisoners entered the magician arose and stood upon his cloven feet, and then silently walked to a curtained archway.

Sacho commanded the prisoners to follow, and beyond the archway they found a vast chamber that occupied the center of the castle and was as big as a ballroom. Zog, who seemed to walk with much difficulty because his ungainly body swayed back and forth, did not go far beyond the arched entrance. A golden throne was set near by, and in this the monster seated himself.

At one side of the throne stood a group of slaves. They were men, women and children. All had broad gold bands clasped around their ankles, as a badge of servitude, and at each throat were the fish's gills that enabled them to breathe, and live under water. Yet every face was smiling and serene, even in the presence of their dread master. In parts of the big hall were groups of other slaves.

Sacho ranged the prisoners in a circle before Zog's throne, and slowly the magician turned his eyes, glowing like live coals, upon the four.

"Captives," said he, speaking in his clear, sweet voice, "in our first interview you defied me, and both the mermaid queen and the princess declared they could not die. But if

that is a true statement, as I have yet to discover, there are various ways to make you miserable and unhappy, and this I propose to do in order to amuse myself at your expense.

Chapter Fifteen

You have been brought here to undergo the first trial of strength between us."

None of the prisoners replied to this speech, so Zog turned to one of his slaves and said:

"Rivivi, bring in the Yell-Maker."

Rivivi was a big fellow, brown of skin, and with flashing black eyes. He bowed to his master and left the room by

an archway covered with heavy draperies. The next moment these curtains were violently pushed aside and a dreadful sea creature swam into the hall. It had a body much like that of a crab, only more round and of a jet-black color. Its eyes were bright yellow balls set on the ends of two horns that stuck out of its head. They were cruel looking eyes, too, and seemed able to see every person in the room at the same time.

The legs of the Yell-Maker, however, were the most curious part of the creature. There were six of them, slender and black as coal, and each extended twelve to fifteen feet from its body, when stretched out in a straight line. They were hinged in several places, so they could be folded up, or extended at will. At the ends of these thin legs were immense claws shaped like those of a lobster, and they were real "nippers," of a most dangerous sort.

The prisoners knew, as soon as they saw the awful claws, why the thing was called the "Yell-Maker," and Trot gave a little shiver and crept closer to Cap'n Bill.

Zog looked with approval upon the creature he had summoned, and said to it:

"I give you four victims—the four people with fish's tails. Let me hear how loud they can yell."

The Yell-Maker uttered a grunt of pleasure and in a flash stretched out one of its long legs toward the queen's nose, where its powerful claws came together with a loud snap. Aquareine did not stir; she only smiled. Both Zog and the creature that had attacked her seemed much surprised to find she was unhurt.

"Again!" cried Zog; and again the Yell-Maker's claw shot out and tried to pinch the queen's pretty ear. But the magic of the fairy mermaid was proof against this sea-rascal's strength and swiftness, nor could he touch any part of Aquareine, although he tried again and again, roaring with anger like a mad bull.

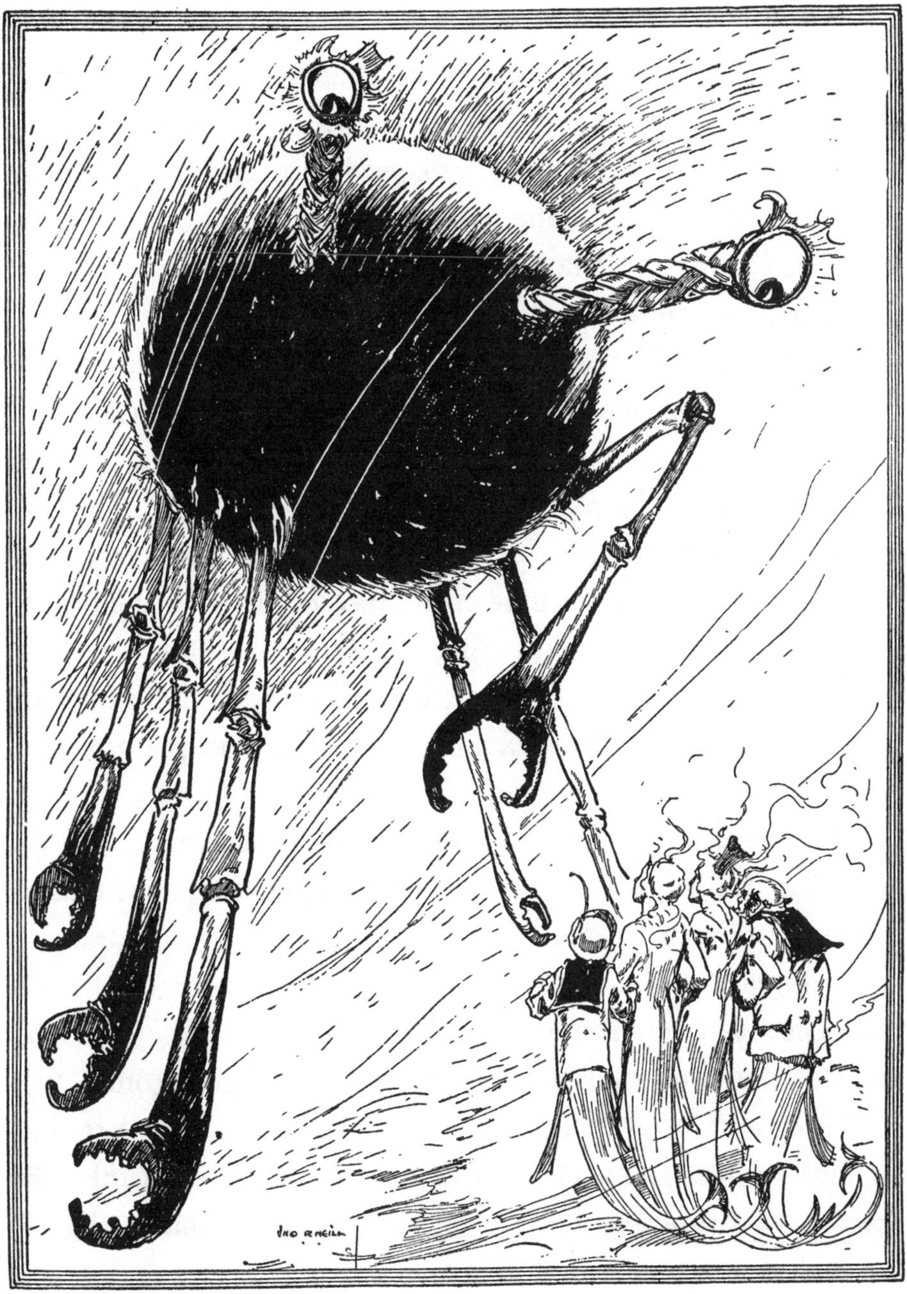
JNO R NEILL

Trot began to enjoy this performance, and as her merry, childish laughter rang out the Yell-Maker turned furiously upon the little girl, two of the dreadful claws trying to nip her at the same time. She had no chance to cry out, or jump backward; yet she remained unharmed. For the Fairy Circle of Queen Aquareine kept her safe.

Now Cap'n Bill was attacked, and Princess Clia as well. The half-dozen slender legs darted in every direction, like sword thrusts, to reach their victims, and the cruel claws snapped so rapidly that the sound was like the rattling of castanets. But the four prisoners regarded their enemy with smiling composure, and no yell greeted the Yell-Maker's efforts.

"Enough!" said Zog, softly and sweetly. "You may retire, my poor Yell-Maker, for with these people you are powerless."

The creature paused, and rolled its yellow eyes.

"May I nip just one of the slaves, oh, Zog?" it asked, pleadingly. "I hate to leave without pleasing your ears with a single yell."

"Let my slaves alone," was Zog's answer. "They are here to serve me, and must not be injured. Go, feeble one!"

"Not so!" cried the Queen. "It is a shame, Zog, that such an evil thing should exist in our fair sea." With this, she drew her fairy wand from a fold of her gown and waved it

Chapter Fifteen

toward the creature. At once, the Yell-Maker sank down unconscious upon the floor; its legs fell apart in many pieces, the claws tumbling in a heap beside the body. Then all grew withered and lost shape, becoming a pulpy mass, like gelatine. A few moments later the creature had melted away to nothing

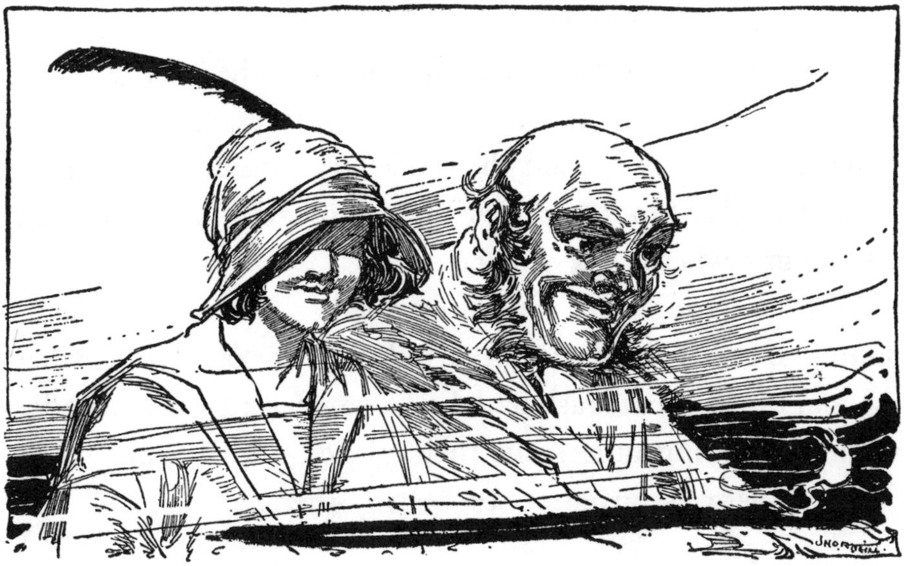

at all, forever disappearing from the ocean where it had caused so much horror and pain.

Zog watched this destruction with surprising patience. When it was all over he nodded his head and smiled, and Trot noticed that whenever Zog smiled his slaves lost their jolly looks and began to tremble.

"That is very pretty magic, Aquareine," said the monster. "I, myself, learned the trick several thousand years ago, so it does not astonish me. Have you fairies nothing that is new to show me?"

"We desire only to protect ourselves," replied the Queen. with dignity.

"Then I will give you a chance to do so," said Zog.

As he spoke the great marble blocks in the ceiling of the room, directly over the heads of the captives, gave way and came crashing down upon them. Many tons of weight were in these marble blocks, and the magician had planned to crush his victims where they stood.

But the four were still unharmed. The marble, being unable to touch them, was diverted from its course, and when the roar of the great crash had died away Zog saw his intended victims standing quietly in their places, and smiling scornfully at his weak attempts to destroy them.

The TOP OF THE GREAT DOME

Chap. 16

CAP'N BILL'S heart was beating pretty fast, but he did not let Zog know that. Trot was so sure of the protection of the fairy mermaids that she would not allow herself to become frightened. Aquareine and Clia were as calm as if nothing had happened.

"Please excuse this little interruption," said Zog. "I knew very well the marble blocks could not hurt you. But the play is over for a time. You may now retire to your rooms, and when I again invite you to my presence I shall have found some better way to entertain you."

Without reply to this threat they turned and followed Sacho from the hall, and the boy led them straight back to their own rooms.

"Zog is making a great mistake," said Sacho, with a laugh.

179

"He has no time for vengeance, but the great magician does not know that."

"What is he trying to do, anyway?" asked Trot.

"He does not tell me his secrets, but I've an idea he wants to kill you," replied Sacho. "How absurd it is to be plotting such a thing, when he might spend his time in laughing and being jolly! Isn't it, now?"

"Zog is a wicked, wicked, creature!" exclaimed Trot.

"But he has his good points," replied Sacho, cheerfully. "There is no one in all the world so bad that there is nothing good about him."

"I'm not so sure of that," said Cap'n Bill. "What are Zog's good points?"

"All his slaves were saved from drowning, and he is kind to them," said Sacho.

"That is merely the kindness of selfishness," said Aquareine. "Tell me, my lad, is the opening in the great dome outside, guarded?"

"Yes, indeed," was the reply. "You cannot hope to escape in that way, for the prince of the sea devils, who is the largest and fiercest of his race, lies crouched over the opening, night and day, and none can pass his network of curling legs."

"Is there no avenue that is not guarded?" continued Aquareine.

Chapter Sixteen

"None at all, your Majesty. Zog is always careful to be well guarded, for he fears the approach of an enemy. What this enemy can be, to terrify the powerful magician, I do not know; but Zog is always afraid and never leaves an entrance unguarded. Besides, it is an enchanted castle, you know, and none in the ocean can see it unless Zog wishes him to. So it will be very hard for his enemy to find him."

"We wish to escape," said Clia. "Will **you help us,** Sacho?"

"In any way I can," replied the boy.

"If we succeed, we will take you with us," continued the Princess. But Sacho shook his head, and laughed.

"I would indeed like to see you escape Zog's vengeance," said he, "for vengeance is wrong and you are too pretty, and too good to be destroyed. But I am happy here, and have no wish to go away, having no other home or friends, other than my fellow slaves."

Then he left them, and when they were again alone, Aquareine said:

"We were able to escape Zog's attacks to-day, but I am quite sure he will plan more powerful ways to destroy us. He has shown that he knows some clever magic and perhaps I shall not be able to foil it. So it will be well for us to escape to-night, if possible."

"Can you fight and conquer the big sea devil up in the dome?" asked Trot.

The queen was thoughtful, and did not reply to this question at once. But Cap'n Bill said, uneasily:

"I can't abide them devil critters, an' I hopes, for my part, we won't be called on to tackle 'em. You see, Trot, we're in consider'ble of a bad mess, an' if we ever live to tell the tale—"

"Why not, Cap'n?" asked the child. "We're safe enough, so far. Can't you trust to our good friend the queen?"

"She don't seem plumb sure o' things herself," remarked the sailor. "The mermaids is all right an' friendly, mate, but this 'ere magic maker—ol' Zog—is a bad one, out 'n' out, an' means to kill us, if he can."

"But he can't!" cried Trot, bravely.

"I hope you're right, dear. I wouldn't want to bet on Zog's chances, jes' yet, an' at the same time it would be riskin' money to bet on our chances. Seems to me it's a case of luck which wins."

"Don't worry, friend," said the Queen. "I have a plan to save us. Let us wait patiently until nightfall."

They waited in the Rose Chamber a long time, talking earnestly together; but the brilliant light that flooded both the room and the great dome outside did not fade in the least.

After several hours had passed away the gong sounded

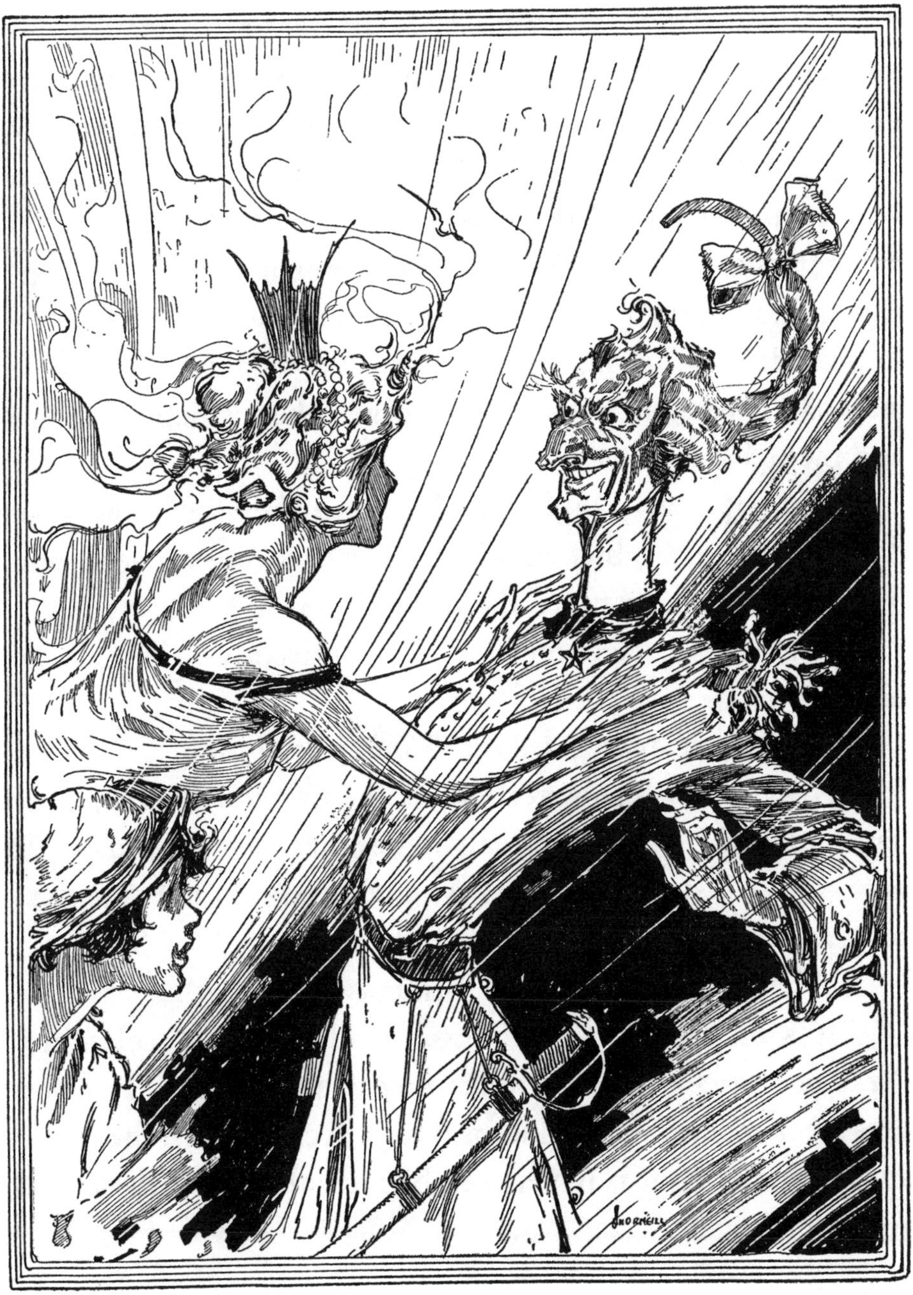

and Tom Atto again appeared, followed by four slaves bearing many golden dishes upon silver trays. The friendly cook had prepared a fine dinner and they were all glad to find that, whatever Zog intended to do to them, he had no intention of starving them. Perhaps the magician realized that Aquareine's fairy powers, if put to the test, would be able to provide food for her companions; but whatever his object may have been, their enemy had given them splendid rooms and plenty to eat.

"Isn't it nearly night time?" asked the Queen, as Tom Atto spread the table with a cloth of woven seaweed and directed his men to place the dishes upon it.

"Night!" he exclaimed, as if surprised. "There is no night here."

"Doesn't it ever get dark?" inquired Trot.

"Never. We know nothing of the passage of time, or of day and night. The light always shines just as you see it now, and we sleep whenever we are tired and rise again as soon as we are rested."

"What causes the light?" Princess Clia asked.

"It's magic, your Highness," said the cook, solemnly. "It's one of the curious things Zog is able to do. But you must remember all this place is a big cave, in which the castle stands, so the light is never seen by anyone, except those who live here."

Chapter Sixteen

"But why does Zog keep his light going all the time?" asked the Queen.

"I suppose it is because he himself never sleeps," replied Tom Atto. "They say the master has n't slept for hundreds of years; not since Anko, the sea serpent, defeated him and drove him into this place."

They asked no more questions, and began to eat their dinner in silence. Before long Cap'n Joe came in to visit his brother, and took a seat at the table with the prisoners. He proved a jolly fellow, and when he and Cap'n Bill talked about their boyhood days the stories were so funny that everybody laughed, and for a time forgot their worries.

The Sea Fairies

When dinner was over, however, and Cap'n Joe had gone back to his work of sewing on buttons and the servants had carried away the dishes, the prisoners remembered their troubles and the fate that awaited them.

"I am much disappointed," said the Queen, "to find there is no night here, and that Zog never sleeps. It will make our escape more difficult. Yet we must make the attempt, and as we are tired and a great struggle is before us, it will be best for us to sleep and refresh ourselves."

They agreed to this, for the day had been long and adventurous, so Cap'n Bill kissed Trot and went into the Peony Room, where he lay down upon his spongy couch and soon fell fast asleep.

The mermaids and Trot followed this example, and I think none of them was much worried, after all, because they quickly sank into peaceful slumber and forgot all the dangers that threatened them.

The QUEEN'S GOLDEN SWORD

Chap 17.

"GOODNESS me!" exclaimed Trot, raising herself by a flirt of her pink-scaled tail and a wave of her fins; "is n't it dreadful hot here?"

The mermaids had risen at the same time, and Cap'n Bill came swimming in from the Peony Room in time to hear the little girl's speech.

"Hot!" echoed the sailor, "why, I feel like the inside of a steam engine!"

The perspiration was rolling down his round, red face, and he took out his handkerchief and carefully wiped it away, waving his fishtail gently at the same time.

"What we need most in this room," said he, "is a fan."

"What's the trouble, do you s'pose?" inquired Trot.

"It is another trick of the monster Zog," answered the Queen, calmly. "He has made the water in our rooms boiling hot, and if it could touch us we would be well cooked by this time. Even as it is, we are all made uncomfortable by breathing the heated air."

"What shall we do, ma'am?" the sailorman asked, with a groan. "I expected to get into hot water afore we 've done with this foolishness, but I don't like the feel o' bein' parboiled, jes' the same."

The queen was waving her fairy wand, and paid no attention to Cap'n Bill's moans. Already, the water felt cooler and they began to breathe more easily. In a few moments more the heat had passed from the surrounding water altogether, and all danger from this source was over.

"This is better," said Trot, gratefully.

"Do you care to sleep again?" asked the Queen.

"No; I 'm wide awake, now," answered the child.

"I 'm afraid if I goes to sleep ag'in I 'll wake up a pot roast," said Cap'n Bill.

"Let us consider ways to escape," suggested Clia. "It seems useless for us to remain here, quietly, until Zog discovers a way to destroy us."

"But we must not blunder," added Aquareine, cautiously. "To fail in our attempt would be to acknowledge Zog's superior power, so we must think well upon our plan before we begin to carry it out. What do you advise, sir?" she asked, turning to Cap'n Bill.

"My opinion, ma'am, is that the only way for us to escape is to get out o' here," was the sailor's vague answer. "How to do it is your business, seein' as I ain't no fairy myself, either in looks or in eddication."

The queen smiled, and said to Trot:

"What is your opinion, my dear?"

"I think we might swim out the same way we came in," answered the child. "If we could get Sacho to lead us back through the maze, we would follow that long tunnel to the open ocean, and—"

"And there would be the sea devils waitin' for us," added Cap'n Bill, with a shake of his bald head. "They'd drive us back inter the tunnel, like they did the first time, Trot. It won't do, mate; it won't do."

"Have you a suggestion, Clia?" inquired the Queen.

"I have thought of an undertaking," replied the pretty princess; "but it is a bold plan, your Majesty, and you may not care to risk it."

"Let us hear it, anyway," said Aquareine, encouragingly.

"It is to destroy Zog himself, and put him out of the world forever. Then we would be free to go home, whenever we pleased."

"Can you suggest a way to destroy Zog?" asked Aquareine.

"No, your Majesty," Clia answered. "I must leave the way for you to determine."

"In the old days," said the Queen, thoughtfully, "the mighty King Anko could not destroy this monster. He succeeded in defeating Zog, and drove him into this great cavern; but even Anko could not destroy him."

"I have heard the sea serpent explain that it was because he could not reach the magician," returned Clia. "If King Anko could have seized Zog in his coils he would have made an end of the wicked monster quickly. Zog knows this, and that is why he does not dare to venture forth from his retreat. Anko is the enemy he constantly dreads. But with you, my queen, the case is different. You may easily reach Zog, and the only question is whether your power is sufficient to destroy him."

For a while, Aquareine remained silent.

"I am not sure of my power over Zog," she said at last, "and for that reason I hesitate to attack him personally. His slaves, and his allies the sea devils, I can easily conquer; so I prefer to find a way to overcome the guards at the entrances, rather than to encounter their terrible master. But even the guards have been given strength and power by the magician, as we have already discovered; so I must procure a weapon with which to fight them."

"A weapon, ma'am?" said Cap'n Bill; and then he took

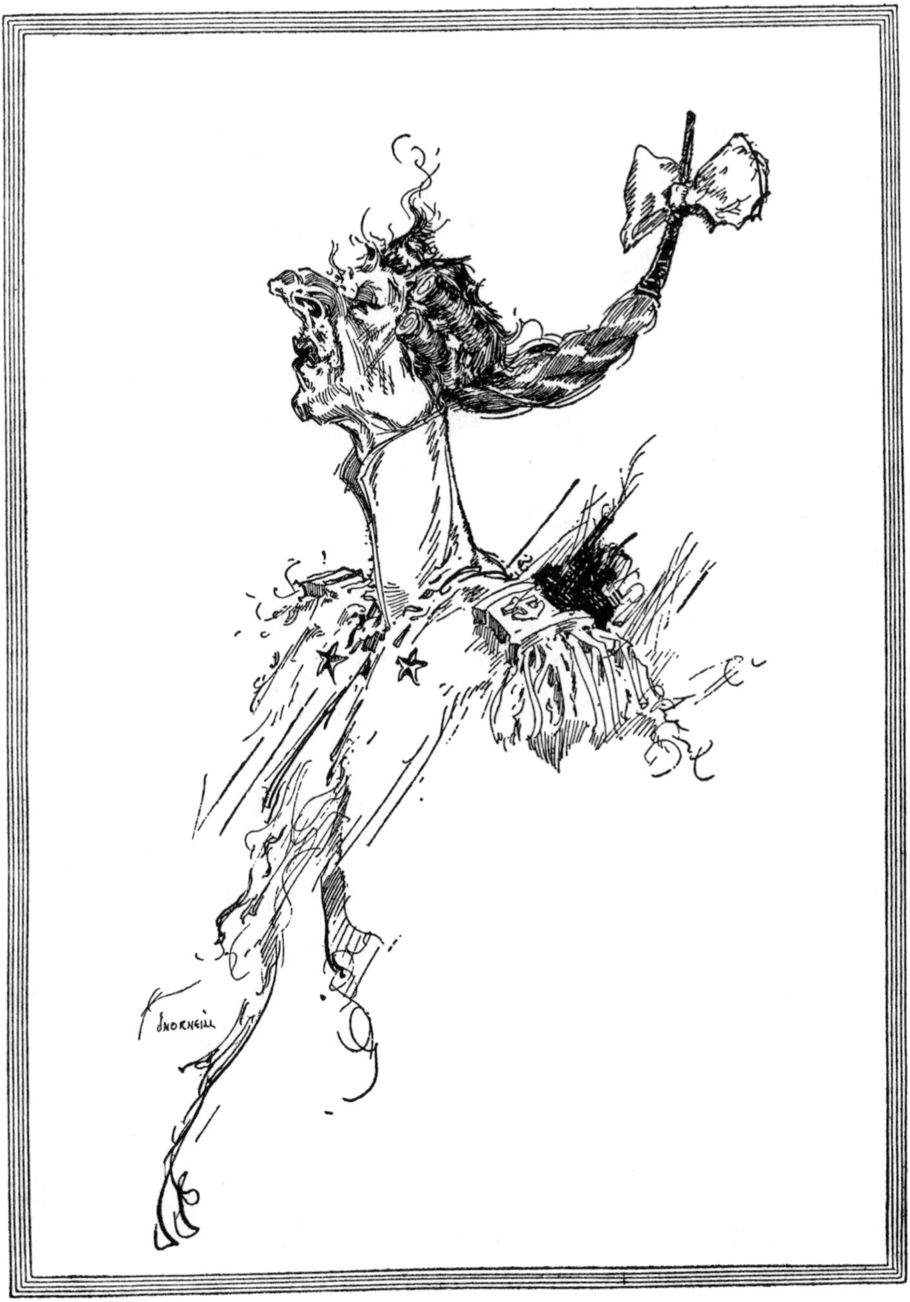

a jackknife from his coat pocket and opened the big blade, afterward handing it to the queen. "That ain't a bad weapon," he announced.

"But it is useless in this case," she replied, smiling at the old sailor's earnestness. "For my purpose I must have a golden sword."

"Well, there's plenty of gold around this castle," said Trot, looking around her. "Even in this room there's enough to make a hundred golden swords."

"But we can't melt or forge gold under water, mate," the Cap'n said.

"Why not? Don't you s'pose all these gold roses and things were made under water?" asked the little girl.

"Like enough," admitted the sailor; "but I don't see how."

Just then, the gong at their door sounded and the boy Sacho came in, smiling and cheerful as ever. He said Zog had sent him to inquire after their health and happiness.

"You may tell him that his water became a trifle too warm, so we cooled it," replied the Queen. Then they told Sacho how the boiling water had made them uncomfortable while they slept.

Sacho whistled a little tune, and seemed thoughtful.

"Zog is foolish," said he. "How often have I told him that vengeance is but a waste of time. He is worried to know how to destroy you, and that is wasting more time. You are worried for fear he will injure you, and so you also are wasting time. My, my! what a waste of time is going on in this castle!"

"Seems to me that we have so much time it does n't matter," said Trot. "What's time for, anyhow?"

"Time is given us to be happy, and for no other reason," replied the boy, soberly. "When we waste time, we waste happiness. But there is no time for preaching, so I'll go."

"Please wait a moment, Sacho," said the Queen.

"Can I do anything to make you happy?" he asked, smiling again.

"Yes," answered Aquareine. "We are curious to know who does all this beautiful gold work and ornamentation."

"Some of the slaves here are goldsmiths, having been taught by Zog to forge and work metal under water," explained Sacho. "In parts of the ocean lie many rocks filled with veins of pure gold and golden nuggets, and we get large supplies from sunken ships, as well. There is no lack of gold here, but it is not as precious as it is upon the earth, because here we have no need of money."

"We would like to see the goldsmiths at work," announced the Queen.

The boy hesitated a moment. Then he said:

"I will take you to their room, where you may watch them

for a time. I will not ask Zog's permission to do this, for he might refuse. But my orders were to allow you the liberty of the castle, and so I will let you see the goldsmiths' shop."

"Thank you," replied Aquareine, quietly; and then the four followed Sacho along various corridors until they came to a large room, where a dozen men were busily at work. The shop was flooded with the brilliant, unknown light. Lying here and there were heaps of virgin gold, some in its natural state and some already fashioned into ornaments and furniture of various sorts. Each man worked at a bench where there was a curious iron furnace in which glowed a vivid, white light. Although this workshop was all under water, and the workmen were obliged to breathe as fishes do, the furnaces glowed so hot that the water touching them was turned into steam. Gold, or other metal, held over a furnace quickly softened or melted, when it could be forged or molded into any shape desired.

"The furnaces are electric," explained Sacho, "and heat as well under water as they would in the open air. Let me introduce you to the foreman, who will tell you of his work better than I can."

The foreman was a slave named Agga-Groo, who was lean and lank, and had an expression more surly and unhappy than any slave they had yet seen. Yet he seemed willing to leave his work and explain to the visitors how he made so many

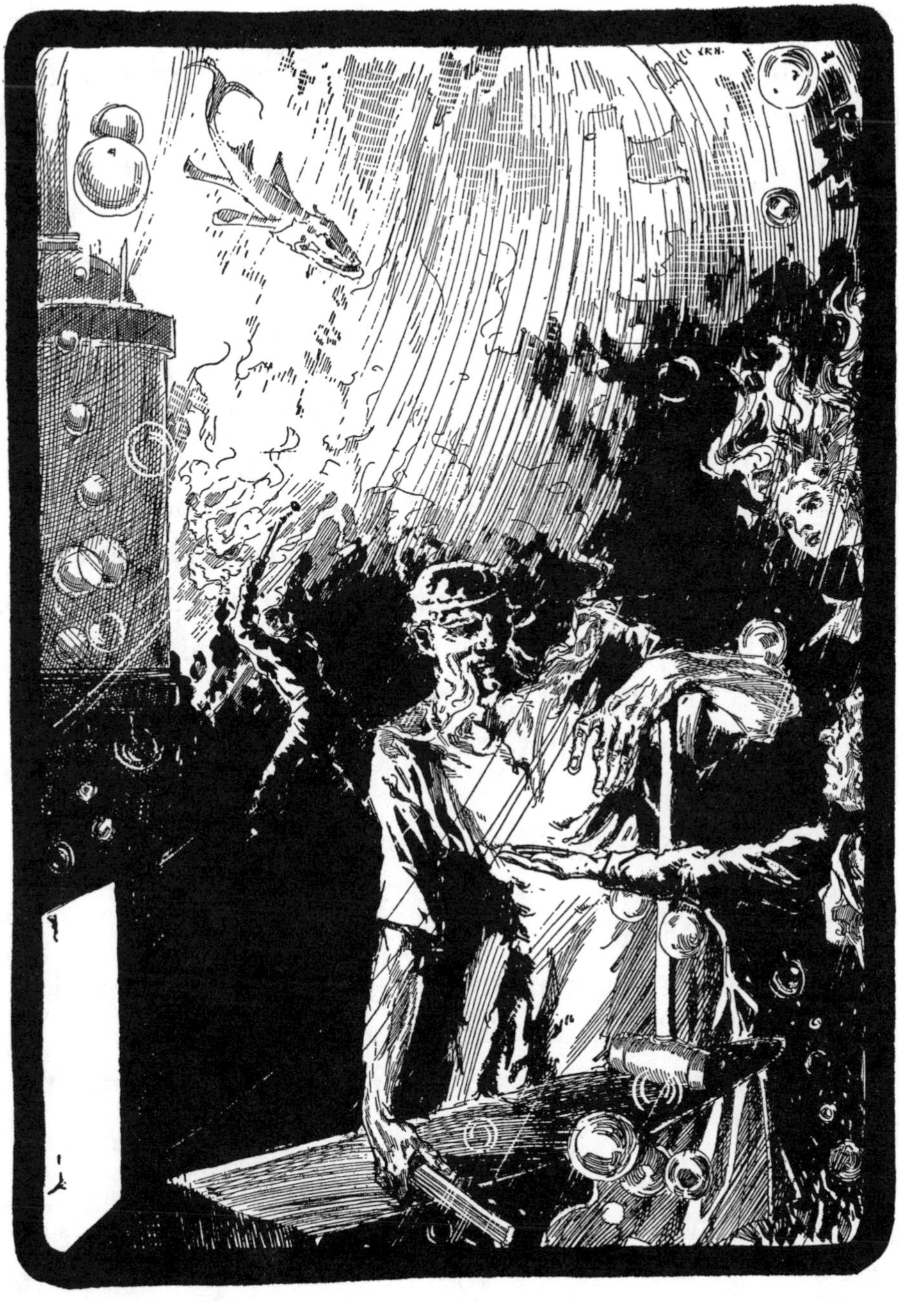

beautiful things out of gold, for he took much pride in this labor and knew its artistic worth. Moreover, since he had been in Zog's castle, these were the first strangers to enter his workshop, so he welcomed them in his own gruff way.

The queen asked him if he was happy, and he shook his head and replied:

"It is n't like Calcutta, where I used to work in gold before I was wrecked at sea, and nearly drowned. Zog rescued me and brought me here a slave. It is a stupid life we lead, doing the same things over and over every day; but perhaps it is better than being dead. I 'm not sure. The only pleasure I get in life is in creating pretty things out of gold."

"Could you forge me a golden sword?" asked the Queen, smiling sweetly upon the goldsmith.

"I could, madam; but I won't unless Zog orders me to do it."

"Do you like Zog better than you do me?" inquired Aquareine.

"No," was the answer. "I hate Zog."

"Then won't you make the sword to please me—and to show your skill?" pleaded the pretty mermaid.

"I 'm afraid of my master. He might not like it," the man replied.

"But he will never know," said Princess Clia.

"You cannot say what Zog knows; or what he does n't

know," growled the man. "I can't take chances of offending Zog, for I must live with him always as a slave."

With this he turned away and resumed his work, hammering the leaf of a golden tulip.

Cap'n Bill had listened carefully to this conversation, and being a wise old sailor, in his way, he thought he understood the nature of old Agga-Groo better than the mermaids did. So he went close to the goldsmith, and feeling in the pockets of his coat drew out a silver compass, shaped like a watch.

"I'll give you this, if you'll make the queen the golden sword," he said.

Agga-Groo looked at the compass with interest, and tested its power of pointing north. Then he shook his head, and handed it back to Cap'n Bill.

The sailor dived into his pocket again and pulled out a pair of scissors, which he placed beside the compass on the palm of his big hand.

"You may have them both," he said.

Agga-Groo hesitated, for he wanted the scissors badly; but finally he shook his head again. Cap'n Bill added a piece of cord, an iron thimble, some fishhooks, four buttons, and a safety pin; but, still the goldsmith would not be tempted. So, with a sigh, the sailor brought out his fine, big jackknife, and at sight of this Agga-Groo's eyes began to sparkle. Steel was not to be had at the bottom of the sea, although gold was so plentiful.

"All right, friend," he said; "give me that lot of trinkets and I'll make you a pretty gold sword. But it won't be any good except to look at, for our gold is so pure that it is very soft."

"Never mind that," replied Cap'n Bill. "All we want is the sword."

The goldsmith set to work at once, and so skillful was he that in a few minutes he had forged a fine sword of yellow gold, with an ornamental handle. The shape was graceful, and the blade keen and slender.

It was evident to them all that the golden sword would not stand hard use, for the edge of the blade would nick and curl like lead; but the queen was delighted with the prize, and took it eagerly in her hand.

Just then Sacho returned to say that they must go back to their rooms, and after thanking the goldsmith, who was so busy examining his newly-acquired treasures that he made no response, they joyfully followed the boy back to the Rose Chamber.

Sacho told them that he had just come from Zog, who was still wasting time in plotting vengeance.

"You must be careful," he advised them, "for my cruel master intends to stop you from living, and he may succeed. Don't be unhappy; but be careful. Zog is angry because you escaped his Yell-Maker, and the falling stones, and the hot

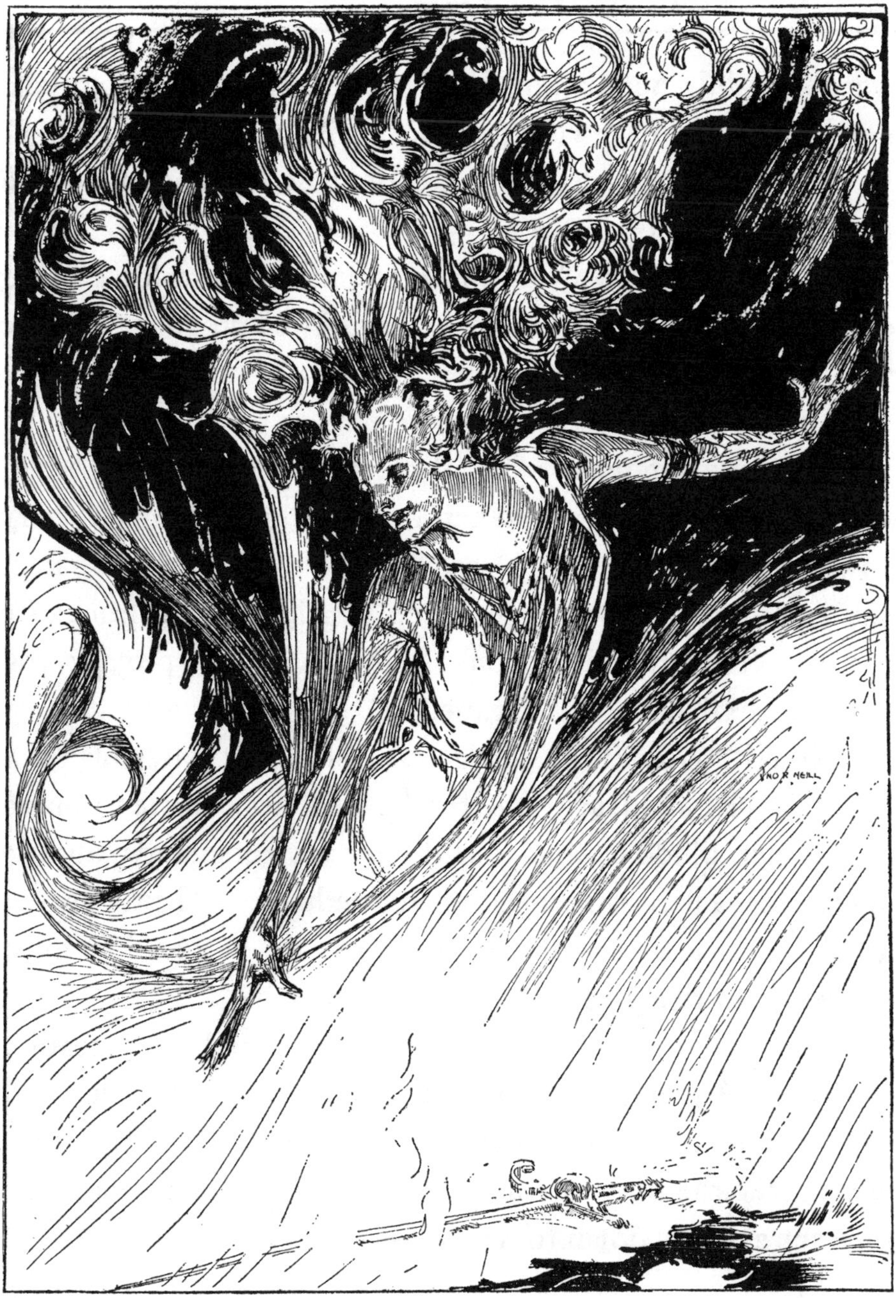
JNO R NEILL

water. While he is angry he is wasting time; but that will not help you. Take care not to waste any time yourselves."

"Do you know what Zog intends to do to us next?" asked Princess Clia.

"No," said Sacho; "but it is reasonable to guess that, being evil, he intends evil. He never intends to do good, I assure you."

Then the boy went away.

"I am no longer afraid," declared the Mermaid Queen, when they were alone. "When I have bestowed certain fairy powers upon this golden sword, it will fight its way against any who dare oppose us, and even Zog himself will not care to face so powerful a weapon. I am now able to promise you that we shall make our escape."

"Good!" cried Trot, joyfully. "Shall we start now?"

"Not yet, my dear. It will take me a little while to charm this golden blade so that it will obey my commands, and do my work. There is no need of undue haste, so I propose we all sleep for a time and obtain what rest we can. We must be fresh and ready for our great adventure."

As their former nap had been interrupted, they readily agreed to Aquareine's proposal and at once went to their couches and composed themselves to slumber. When they were asleep the fairy mermaid charmed her golden sword, and then she also lay down to rest herself.

A DASH FOR LIBERTY

Chap. 18

TROT dreamed that she was at home in her own bed; but the night seemed chilly and she wanted to draw the coverlet up to her chin. She was not wide awake, but realized that she was cold and was unable to move her arms to cover herself up. She tried, but could not stir. Then she roused herself a little more, and tried again. Yes; it was cold—very cold! Really, she *must* do something to get warm, she thought. She opened her eyes, and stared at a great wall of ice in front of her.

She was awake now, and frightened, too. But, she could not move because the ice was all around her. She was frozen inside of it, and the air space around her was not big enough to allow her to turn over.

At once, the little girl realized what had happened. Their wicked enemy Zog had, by his magic art, frozen all the water in their room while they slept, and now they were all imprisoned and helpless. Trot and Cap'n Bill were sure to freeze to death in a short time, for only a tiny air space remained between their bodies and the ice, and this air was like that of a winter day when the thermometer is below zero.

Across the room Trot could see the mermaid queen lying on her couch, for the solid ice was clear as crystal. Aquareine was imprisoned just as Trot was, and although she held her fairy wand in one hand and the golden sword in the other, she seemed unable to move either of them, and the girl remembered that the queen always waved her magic wand to accomplish anything. Princess Clia's couch was behind that of Trot, so the child could not see her; and Cap'n Bill was in his own room, probably frozen fast in the ice, as the others were.

The terrible Zog had surely been very clever in this last attempt to destroy them. Trot thought it all over, and decided that, inasmuch as the queen was unable to wave her fairy wand, she could do nothing to release herself or her friends.

But in this the girl was mistaken. The fairy mermaid was even now at work, trying to save them, and in a few minutes Trot was astonished and delighted to see the queen rise from her couch. She could not go far from it, at first, but the ice was melting rapidly all around her; so that gradually Aquareine approached the place where the child lay. Trot could hear the mermaid's voice sounding through the ice, as if from afar off; but it grew more distinct until she could make out that the queen was saying: "Courage, friends! Do not despair, for soon you will be free."

Before very long the ice between Trot and the queen had melted away entirely, and with a cry of joy the little girl flopped her pink tail and swam to the side of her deliverer.

"Are you very cold?" asked Aquareine.

"N—not v—v—very!" replied Trot; but, her teeth chattered and she was still shivering.

"The water will be warm in a few minutes," said the Queen. "But now I must melt the rest of the ice and liberate Clia."

This she did in an astonishingly brief time, and the pretty princess, being herself a fairy, had not been at all affected by the cold surrounding her.

They now swam to the door of Cap'n Bill's room and found the Peony Chamber a solid block of ice. The queen worked her magic power as hard as she could, and the ice thawed and melted quickly before her fairy wand. Yet when they reached the old sailor he was almost frozen stiff, and Trot and Clia had to rub his hands and nose, and ears very briskly to warm him up, and bring him back to life.

Cap'n Bill was pretty tough, and he came around in time and opened his eyes and sneezed, and asked if the blizzard was over. So the queen waved her wand over his head a few times to restore him to his natural condition of warmth, and soon the old sailor became quite comfortable and was able to understand all about the strange adventure from which he had so marvelously escaped.

"I've made up my mind to one thing, Trot," he said confidentially; "if ever I get out o' this mess I'm in, I won't be an Arctic explorer, whatever else happens. Shivers an' shakes ain't to my likin', an' this ice business ain't what it's sometimes cracked up to be. To be friz once is enough fer anybody, an' if I was a gal like you I wouldn't even wear frizzes on my hair."

"You haven't any hair, Cap'n Bill," answered Trot; "so you needn't worry."

The queen and Clia had been talking together very earnestly. They now approached their earth friends, and Aquareine said:

"We have decided not to remain in this castle any longer. Zog's cruel designs upon our lives and happiness are becoming too dangerous for us to endure. The golden sword now bears a fairy charm, and by its aid I will cut a way through our enemies. Are you ready and willing to follow me?"

"Of course we are!" cried Trot.

Chapter Eighteen

"It don't seem 'zactly right to ask a lady to do the fightin'," remarked Cap'n Bill; "but magic ain't my strong p'int, and it seems to be yours, ma'am. So swim ahead, and we 'll wiggle the same way you do, an' try to wiggle out of our troubles."

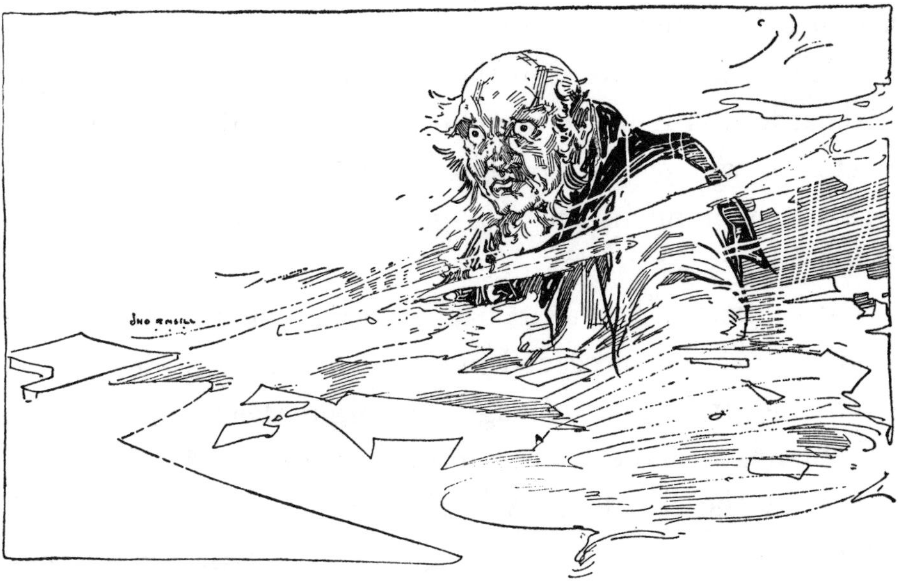

"If I chance to fail," said the Queen, "try not to blame me. I will do all in my power to provide for our escape, and I am willing to risk everything, because I well know that to remain here will mean to perish in the end."

"That 's all right," said Trot, with fine courage. "Let 's have it over with."

"Then we will leave here at once," said Aquareine.

She approached the window of the room, and with one blow of her golden sword shattered the thick pane of glass. The opening thus made was large enough for them to swim through, if they were careful not to scrape against the broken points of glass. The queen went first, followed by Trot and Cap'n Bill, with Clia last of all.

And now they were in the vast dome in which the castle and gardens of Zog had been built. Around them was a clear stretch of water, and far above—full half a mile distant—was the opening in the roof guarded by the prince of the sea devils.

The mermaid queen had determined to attack this monster. If she succeeded in destroying it with her golden sword the little band of fugitives might then swim through the opening into the clear waters of the ocean. Although this prince of the sea devils was said to be big and wise and mighty, there was but one of him to fight; whereas, if they attempted to escape through any of the passages, they must encounter scores of such enemies.

"Swim straight for the opening in the dome!" cried Aquareine, and in answer to the command the four whisked their glittering tails, waved their fins, and shot away through the water at full speed; their course slanting upward toward the top of the dome.

KING ANCO TO THE RESCUE

THE great magician Zog never slept. He was always watchful and alert. Some strange power warned him that his prisoners were about to escape.

Scarcely had the four left the castle by the broken window when the monster stepped from a doorway below and saw them. Instantly he blew upon a golden whistle, and at the summons a band of wolf-fish appeared and dashed after the prisoners. These creatures swam so swiftly that soon they were between the fugitives and the dome, and then they turned and with wicked eyes and sharp fangs began a fierce attack upon the mermaids and the earth dwellers.

Trot was a little frightened at the evil looks of the sea wolves, whose heads were enormous, and whose jaws contained rows of curved and pointed teeth. But, Aquareine advanced upon them with her golden sword and every touch

of the charmed weapon instantly killed an enemy; so, that
one by one the wolf-fish rolled over upon their backs and
sank helplessly downward through the water, leaving the
prisoners free to continue their way toward the opening in
the dome.

Zog witnessed the destruction of his wolves and uttered
a loud laugh that was terrible to hear. Then the dread
monster determined to arrest the fugitives himself, and in
order to do this he was forced to discover himself in all the
horror of his awful form—a form he was so ashamed of and
loathed so greatly that he always strove to keep it concealed,
even from his own eyes. But it was important that his
prisoners should not escape.

Hastily casting off the folds of the robe that enveloped
him Zog allowed his body to uncoil and shoot upward through
the water, in swift pursuit of his victims. His cloven hoofs,
upon which he usually walked, being now useless, were
drawn up under him, while coil after coil of his eel-like body
wriggled away like a serpent. At his shoulders two broad
feathery wings expanded, and these enabled the monster to
cleave his way through the water with terrific force.

Zog was part man, part beast, part fish, part fowl, and
part reptile. His undulating body was broad and thin, and
like the body of an eel. It was as repulsive as one could well

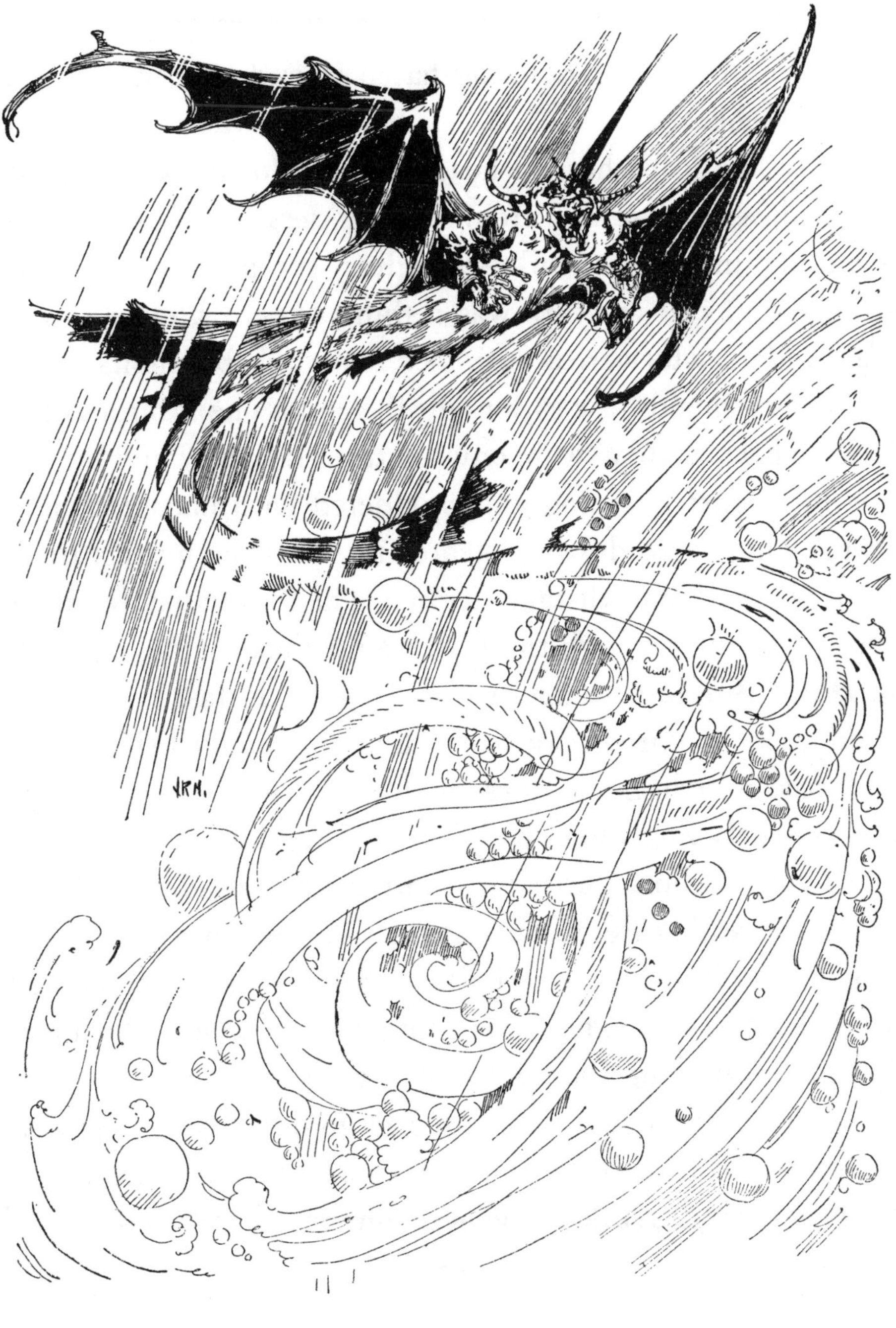
VRH.

imagine, and no wonder Zog hated it and kept it covered with his robe.

Now, with his horned head and its glowing eyes thrust forward, wings flapping from his shoulders and his eely body —ending in a fish's tail—wriggling far behind him, this strange and evil creature was a thing of terror, even to the sea dwellers, who were accustomed to remarkable sights.

The mermaids, the sailor and the child, one after another looking back as they swam onward toward liberty and safety, saw the monster coming and shuddered with uncontrollable fear. They were drawing nearer to the dome by this time, yet it was still some distance away. The four redoubled their speed, darting through the water with the swiftness of sky-rockets. But fast as they swam, Zog swam faster, and the good queen's heart began to throb as she realized she would be forced to fight her loathesome foe.

Presently Zog's long body was circling round them like a whirlwind, lashing the water into foam and gradually drawing nearer and nearer to his victims. His eyes were no longer glowing coals—they were balls of flame—and as he circled around them, he laughed aloud that horrible laugh which was far more terrifying than any cry of rage could be.

The queen struck out with her golden sword, but Zog wrapped a coil of his thin body around it and, wresting it from her hand, crushed the weapon into a shapeless mass.

Chapter Nineteen

Then, Aquareine waved her fairy wand; but, in a flash the monster sent it flying away through the water.

Cap'n Bill now decided that they were lost. He drew Trot closer to his side and placed one arm around her.

"I can't save you, dear little mate," he said, sadly, "but we've lived a long time together, an' now we'll die together. I knew, Trot, when first we sawr them mermaids, as we'd— we'd—"

"Never live to tell the tale," said the child. "But never mind, Cap'n Bill; we've done the best we could, and we've had a fine time."

"Forgive me! oh, forgive me!" cried Aquareine, despairingly. "I tried to save you, my poor friends, but—"

"What's that?" exclaimed the Princess, pointing upward.

They all looked past Zog's whirling body, which was slowly enveloping them in its folds, toward the round opening in the dome. A dark object had appeared there, sliding downward like a huge rope and descending toward them with lightning rapidly. They gave a great gasp as they recognized the countenance of King Anko, the sea serpent, its gray hair and whiskers bristling like those of an angry cat and the usually mild blue eyes glowing with a ferocity even more terrifying than the orbs of Zog.

The magician gave a shrill scream at sight of his dreaded enemy, and abandoning his intended victims Zog made a quick dash to escape. But nothing in the sea could equal the strength and quickness of King Anko when he was roused. In a flash the sea serpent had caught Zog fast in his coils, and his mighty body swept round the monster and imprisoned him tightly.

The four, so suddenly rescued, swam away to a safer distance from the struggle, and then they turned to watch the encounter between the two great opposing powers of the ocean's depths. Yet there was no desperate fight to observe, for the combatants were unequal. The end came before they were aware of it. Zog had been taken by surprise and his great fear of Anko destroyed all of his magic power. When the sea serpent slowly released those awful coils, a mass of jelly-like pulp floated downward through the water, with no remnant of life remaining in it—no form to show it had once been Zog, the Magician.

Then Anko shook his body, that the water might cleanse it, and advanced his head toward the group of four whom he had so opportunely rescued.

"It is all over, friends," said he in his gentle tones, while a mild expression once more reigned on his comical features; "you may go home at any time you please, for the way through the dome will be open as soon as I get my own body through it."

Indeed, so amazing was the length of the great sea serpent,

that only a part of him had descended through the hole into the dome. Without waiting for the thanks of those he had rescued he swiftly retreated to the ocean above, and with grateful hearts they followed him, glad to leave the cavern where they had endured so much anxiety and danger.

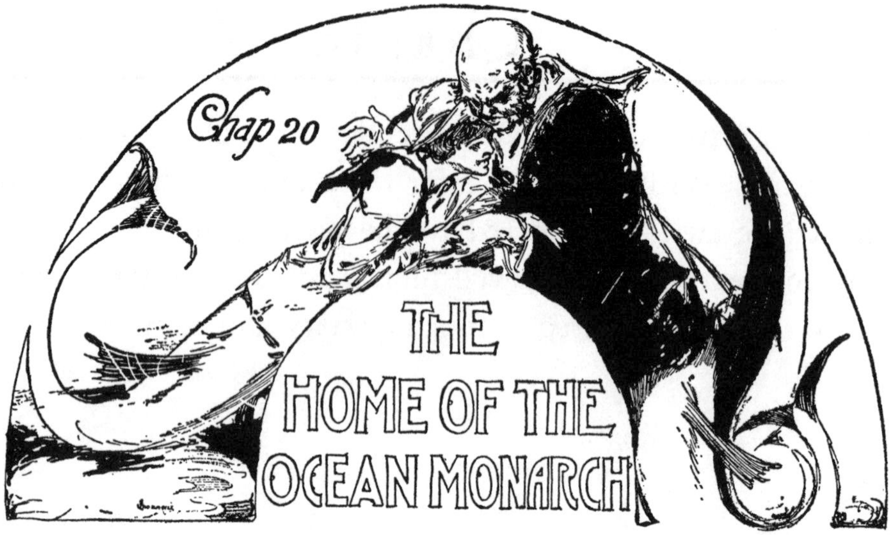
Chap 20
THE
HOME OF THE
OCEAN MONARCH

TROT sobbed quietly, with her head on Cap'n Bill's shoulder. She had been a brave little girl during the trying times they had experienced, and never once had she given way to tears, however desperate their fate had seemed to be. But now that the one enemy in all the sea to be dreaded was utterly destroyed, and all dangers were past, the reaction was so great that she could not help having "just one good cry," as she naively expressed it.

Cap'n Bill was a big sailorman, hardened by age and many adventures; but even he felt a "lump in his throat" that he could not swallow, try as hard as he might. Cap'n Bill was glad. He was mostly glad on Trot's account, for he loved his sweet, childish companion very dearly, and did not want any harm to befall her.

They were now in the wide, open sea, with liberty to go

wherever they wished, and if Cap'n Bill could have "had his say" he would have gone straight home and carried Trot to her mother. But the mermaids must be considered. Aquareine and Clia had been true and faithful friends to their earth guests while dangers were threatening, and it would not be very gracious to leave them at once. Moreover, King Anko was now with them, his big head keeping pace with the mermaids as they swam, and this mighty preserver had a distinct claim upon both Trot and Cap'n Bill. The sailor felt that it would not be polite to ask to go home so soon.

"If you people had come to visit me, as I invited you to do," said the Sea Serpent, "all this bother and trouble would have been saved. I had my palace all put in order to receive the earth dwellers, and sat in my den waiting patiently to receive you. Yet you never came at all."

"That reminds me," said Trot, drying her eyes; "you never told us about that third pain you once had."

"Finally," continued Anko, "I sent to inquire as to what had become of you, and Merla said you had been gone from the palace a long time, and she was getting anxious about you. Then I made inquiries. Every one in the sea loves to serve me—except those sea devils and their cousins the octopi —and it was n't long before I heard you had been captured by Zog."

"Was the third pain as bad as the other two?" asked Trot.

The Sea Fairies

"Naturally, this news disturbed me and made me unhappy," said Anko; "for I well knew, my Aquareine, that the magician's evil powers were greater than your own fairy accomplishments. But I had never been able to find Zog's enchanted castle, and so I was at a loss to know how to save you from your dreadful fate. After I had wasted a good deal of time thinking it over, I decided that if the sea devils were slaves of Zog, the prince of the sea devils must know where the enchanted castle was located.

"I knew this prince, and where to find him, for he always lay on a hollow rock, on the bottom of the sea, and never moved from that position. His people brought food to him and took his commands. So I had no trouble in finding this evil prince, and I went to him and asked the way to Zog's castle. Of course he would not tell me. He was even cross and disrespectful—just as I had expected him to be; so I allowed myself to become angry and killed him, thinking he was much better dead than alive. But after the sea devil was destroyed, what was my surprise to find that all these years he had been lying over a round hole in the rock, and covering it with his scarlet body!

"A light shone through this hole, so I thrust my head in and found a great domed cave underneath, with a splendid silver castle built at the bottom. You, my friends, were at that moment swimming toward me as fast as you could come,

Chapter Twenty

and the monster, Zog, my enemy for centuries past, was close behind you.

"Well, the rest of the story you know. I would be angry with all of you for so carelessly getting captured, had the incident not led to the destruction of the one evil genius in all my ocean. I shall rest easier and be much happier, now that Zog is dead. He has defied me for hundreds of years."

"But, about that third pain," said Trot. "If you don't tell us now, I'm afraid that I'll forget to ask you."

"If you should happen to forget, just remind me of it," said Anko, "and I'll be sure to tell you."

While Trot was thinking this over the swimmers drew near to a great circular palace made all of solid alabaster, polished as smooth as ivory. Its roof was a vast dome, for domes seemed to be fashionable in the ocean houses. There were no doors or windows, but instead of these several round holes appeared in different parts of the dome, some being high up and some low down, and some in between. Out of one of these holes, which it just fitted, stretched the long, brown body of the sea serpent. Trot, being astonished at this sight, asked:

"Did n't you take all of you when you went to the cavern, Anko?"

"Nearly all, my dear," was the reply, accompanied by a cheerful smile, for Anko was proud of his great length; "but

217

not quite all. Some of me remained, as usual, to keep house while my head was away. But, I've been coiling up ever since we started back, and you will soon be able to see every inch of me, all together."

Even as he spoke his head slid into the round hole and, at a signal from Aquareine, they all paused outside and waited.

Presently, there came to them four beautiful winged fishes with faces like doll babies. Their long hair and eyelashes were of a purple color, and their cheeks had rosy spots that looked as if they had been painted upon them.

"His Majesty bids you welcome," said one of the doll fishes, in a sweet voice. "Be kind enough to enter the royal palace and our ocean monarch will graciously receive you."

"Seems to me," said Trot to the queen, "these things are putting on airs. Perhaps they don't know we're friends of Anko."

"The king insists on certain formalities when anyone visits him," was Aquareine's reply. "It is right that his dignity should be maintained."

They followed their winged conductors to one of the upper openings, and as they entered it, Aquareine said in a clear voice: "May the glory and power of the ocean king continue forever!"

Then she touched the palm of her hand to her forehead

in token of allegiance, and Clia did the same; so Cap'n Bill and Trot followed suit. The brief ceremony being ended the child looked curiously around to see what the palace of the mighty Anko was like.

An extensive hall, lined with alabaster, was before them. In the floor were five of the round holes. Upon the walls were engraved many interesting scenes of ocean life, all chiseled very artistically by the tusks of walruses, who, Trot was afterward informed, are greatly skilled in such work. A few handsome rugs of woven sea grasses were spread upon the floor; but otherwise the vast hall was bare of furniture.

The doll-faced fishes escorted them to an upper room where a table was set, and here the travelers were invited to refresh themselves. As all four were exceedingly hungry they welcomed the repast, which was served by an army of lobsters in royal purple aprons and caps.

The meal being finished they again descended to the hall, which seemed to occupy all the middle of the building. And now their conductors said:

"His Majesty is ready to receive you in his den."

They swam downward through one of the round holes in the floor and found themselves in a brilliantly lighted chamber, which appeared bigger than all the rest of the palace put together. In the center was the quaint head of King Anko, and around it was spread a great coverlet of purple and gold woven together. This concealed all of his body and stretched from wall to wall of the circular room.

"Welcome, friends!" said Anko, pleasantly. "How do you like my home?"

"It's very grand," replied Trot.

"Just the place for a sea serpent, seems to me," said Cap'n Bill.

"I'm glad you admire it," said the King. "Perhaps I ought to tell you that from this day you four belong to me."

"How's that?" asked the girl, surprised.

"It is a law of the ocean," declared Anko, "that whoever saves any living creature from violent death owns that creature forever afterward—while life lasts. You will realize how just this law is when you remember that had I not saved you from Zog, you would now be dead. The law was suggested by Captain Kid Glove, when he once visited me."

"Do you mean Captain Kidd?" asked Trot, "because, if you do—"

"Give him his full name," said Anko. "Captain Kid Glove was—"

"There's no glove to it," protested Trot. "I ought to know, 'cause I've read about him."

"Did n't it say anything about a glove?" asked Anko.

"Nothing at all. It jus' called him Cap'n Kidd," replied Trot.

"She's right, ol' man," added Cap'n Bill.

"Books," said the Sea Serpent, "are good enough, as far as they go; but it seems to me your earth books don't go far enough. Captain Kid Glove was a gentleman pirate—a kid-glove pirate. To leave off the glove and call him just Kidd is very disrespectful."

"Oh! you told me to remind you of that third pain," said the little girl.

"Which proves my friendship for you," returned the Sea Serpent, blinking his blue eyes thoughtfully. "No one likes to be reminded of a pain, and that third pain was—was—"

"What was it?" asked Trot.

"It was a stomach ache," replied the King, with a sigh.

"What made it?" she inquired.

"Just my carelessness," said Anko. "I'd been away to foreign parts, seeing how the earth people were getting along. I found the Germans dancing the german, and the Dutch making dutch cheese, and the Belgians combing their belgian hares, and the Turks eating turkey, and the Sardinians sardonically pickling sardines. Then I called on the Prince of Whales, and—"

"You mean the Prince of Wales," corrected Trot.

"I mean what I say, my dear. I saw the battlefield where the Bull Run but the Americans did n't, and when I got to

France I paid a napoleon to see Napoleon with his bones apart. He was—"

"Of course, you mean—" Trot was beginning, but the king would not give her a chance to correct him this time.

"He was very hungry for Hungary," he continued, "and was Russian so fast toward the Poles that I thought he'd discover them. So, as I was not accorded a royal welcome, I took French leave and came home again."

"But the pain—"

"On the way home," continued Anko, calmly, "I was a little absent-minded and ate an anchor. There was a long chain attached to it; and as I continued to swallow the anchor I continued to eat the chain. I never realized what I had done until I found a ship on the other end of the chain. Then I bit it off."

"The ship?" asked Trot.

"No; the chain. I did n't care for the ship, as I saw it contained some skippers. On the way home the chain and anchor began to lie heavily on my stomach. I did n't seem to digest them properly, and by the time I got to my palace, where you will notice there is no throne, I was thrown into throes of severe pain. So I at once sent for Dr. Shark—"

"Are all your doctors sharks?" asked the child.

"Yes; are n't your doctors sharks?" he replied.

"Not all of them," said Trot.

Chapter Twenty

"That is true," remarked Cap'n Bill. "But when you talk of lawyers—"

"I'm not talking of lawyers," said Anko, reprovingly; "I'm talking about my pain. I don't imagine anyone could suffer more than I did with that stomach ache."

"Did you suffer long?" inquired Trot.

"Why, about seven thousand four hundred and eighty-two feet and—"

"I mean a long time."

"It seemed like a long time," answered the King. "Dr. Shark said I ought to put a mustard poultice on my stomach; so I uncoiled myself and summoned my servants, and they began putting on the mustard plaster. It had to be bound all around me, so it wouldn't slip off, and I began to look like an express package. In about four weeks fully one-half of the pain had been covered by the mustard poultice, which got so hot that it hurt me worse than the stomach ache did."

"I know," said Trot. "I had one, once."

"One what?" asked Anko.

"A mustard plaster. They smart pretty bad, but I guess they're a good thing."

"I got myself unwrapped as soon as I could," continued the King, "and then I hunted for the doctor, who hid himself until my anger had subsided. He has never sent in a bill, so I think he must be terribly ashamed of himself."

"You're lucky, sir, to have escaped so easy," said Cap'n Bill. "But you seem pretty well now."

"Yes, I'm more careful of what I eat," replied the Sea Serpent. "But I was saying when Trot interrupted me, that you all belong to me, because I have saved your lives. By the law of the ocean you must obey me in everything."

The sailor scowled a little at hearing this, but Trot laughed, and said:

"The law of the ocean is n't *our* law, 'cause we live on land."

"Just now you are living in the ocean," declared Anko, "and as long as you live here, you must obey my commands."

"What are your commands?" inquired the child.

"Ah; that's the point I was coming to," returned the King, with his comical smile. "The ocean is a beautiful place, and we who belong here love it dearly. In many ways it's a nicer place for a home than the earth, for we have no sunstrokes, mosquitoes, earthquakes or candy shops to bother us. But I am convinced that the ocean is no proper dwelling place for earth people, and I believe the mermaids did an unwise thing when they invited you to visit them."

"I don't," protested the girl. "We've had a fine time; have n't we, Cap'n Bill?"

"Well, it's been diff'rent from what I expected," admitted the sailor.

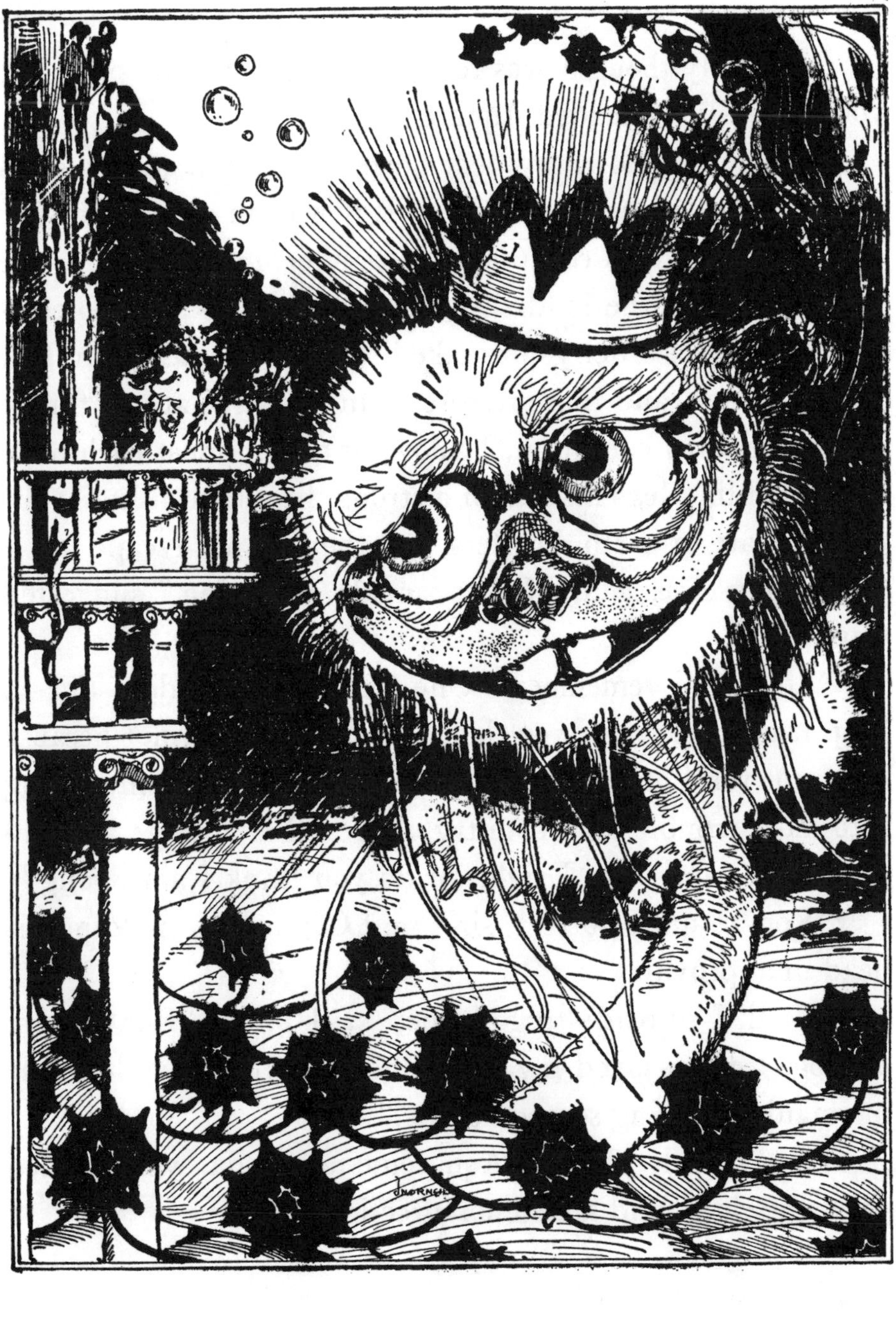

"Our only thought was to give the earth people pleasure, your Majesty," pleaded Aquareine.

"I know; I know, my dear Queen; and it was very good of you," replied Anko. "But, still it was an unwise act, for earth people are as constantly in danger under water as we would be upon the land. So, having won the right to command you all, I order you to take little Mayre and Cap'n Bill straight home, and there restore them to their natural forms. It's a dreadful condition, I know, and they must each have two stumbling legs instead of a strong, beautiful fishtail; but it is the fate of earth dwellers, and they cannot escape it."

"In my case, your Majesty, made it *one* leg," suggested Cap'n Bill.

"Ah, yes; I remember. One leg, and a wooden stick to keep it company. I issue this order, my friends, not because I am not fond of your society, but to keep you from getting into more trouble in a country where all is strange and unnatural to you. Am I right, or do you think I am wrong?"

"You're quite correct, sir," said Cap'n Bill, nodding his head in approval.

"Well, I'm ready to go home," said Trot. "But in spite of Zog, I've enjoyed my visit, and I shall always love the mermaids for being so good to me."

That speech pleased Aquareine and Clia, who smiled upon the child, and kissed her affectionately.

226

Chapter Twenty

"We shall escort you home at once," announced the Queen.

"But before you go," said King Anko, "I will give you a rare treat. It is one you will remember as long as you live. You shall see every inch of the mightiest sea serpent in the world, all at one time!"

As he spoke, the purple and gold cloth was lifted by unseen hands and disappeared from view. And now Cap'n Bill and Trot looked down upon thousands and thousands of coils of the sea serpent's body, which filled all of the space at the bottom of the immense circular room. It reminded them of a great coil of garden hose, only it was so much bigger around, and very much longer.

Except for the astonishing size of the Ocean King, the sight was not an especially interesting one; but they told old Anko that they were pleased to see him, because it was evident he was very proud of his figure.

Then the cloth descended again and covered all but the head; after which they bade the king good-bye and thanked him for all his kindness to them.

"I used to think sea serpents were horrid creatures," said Trot; "but now I know they are good and—and—and—"

"And big," added Cap'n Bill, realizing his little friend could not find another word that was complimentary.

KING JOE

Chap. 21

AS they swam out of Anko's palace and the doll-faced fishes left them, Aquareine asked:

"Would you rather go back to our mermaid home for a time, and rest yourselves, or would you prefer to start for Giant's Cave at once?"

"I guess we'd better go back home," decided Trot. "To our own home, I mean. We've been away quite a while, and King Anko seemed to think it was best."

"Very well," replied the Queen. "Let us turn in this direction, then."

"You can say good-bye to Merla for us," continued Trot. "She was very nice to us, an' 'specially to Cap'n Bill."

"So she was, mate," agreed the sailor; "an' a prettier lady I never knew, even if she is a mermaid, beggin' your pardon, ma'am."

228

Chapter Twenty-one

"Are we going anywhere near Zog's castle?" asked the girl.

"Our way leads directly past the opening in the dome," said Aquareine.

"Then, let's stop and see what Sacho and the others are doing," suggested Trot. "They can't be slaves any longer, you know, 'cause they haven't any master. I wonder if they're any happier than they were before?"

"They seemed to be pretty happy as it was," remarked Cap'n Bill.

"It will do no harm to pay them a brief visit," said Princess Clia. "All danger disappeared from the cavern with the destruction of Zog."

"I really ought to say good-bye to Brother Joe," observed the sailorman. "I won't see him again, you know, and I don't want to seem unbrotherly."

"Very well," said the Queen, "we will reënter the cavern, for I, too, am anxious to know what will be the fate of the poor slaves of the magician."

When they came to the hole in the top of the dome they dropped through it and swam leisurely down toward the castle. The water was clear and undisturbed and the silver castle looked very quiet and peaceful under the radiant light that still filled the cavern.

They met no one at all, and passing around to the front

of the building they reached the broad entrance and passed into the golden hall.

Here a strange scene met their eyes. All the slaves of Zog, hundreds in number, were assembled in the room; while standing before the throne formerly occupied by the wicked magician was the boy Sacho, who was just beginning to make a speech to his fellow slaves.

"At one time or another," he said, "all of us were born upon the earth and lived in the thin air; but now we are all living as the fishes live, and our home is in the water of the ocean. One by one we have come to this place, having been saved from drowning by Zog, the Magician, and by him given power to exist in comfort under water. The powerful master who made us his slaves has now passed away forever, but we continue to live, and are unable to return to our native land, where we would quickly perish. There is no one but us to inherit Zog's possessions, and so it will be best for us to remain in this fine castle and occupy ourselves as we have done before, in providing for the comforts of the community. Only in labor is happiness to be found, and we may as well labor for ourselves as for others.

"But we must have a king. Not an evil, cruel master, like Zog, but one who will maintain order and issue laws for the benefit of all. We will govern ourselves most happily by having a ruler, or head, selected from among ourselves by popular vote. Therefore, I ask you to decide who shall be our king, for only one who is accepted by all can sit in Zog's throne."

The slaves applauded this speech, but they seemed puzzled to make the choice of a ruler. Finally the chief cook came forward and said:

"We all have our duties to perform, and so cannot spend the time to be king. But you, Sacho, who were Zog's own attendant, have now no duties at all. So it will be best for you to rule us. What say you, comrades? Shall we make Sacho king?"

"Yes, yes!" they all cried.

"But I do not wish to be king," replied Sacho. "A king is a useless sort of person, who merely issues orders for others to carry out. I want to be busy and useful. Whoever is king will need a good attendant, as well as an officer who will see that his commands are obeyed. I am used to such duties, having served Zog in this same way."

"Who, then, has the time to rule over us?" asked Agga-Groo, the goldsmith.

"It seems to me that Cap'n Joe is the proper person for king," replied Sacho. "His former duty was to sew buttons on Zog's garments; so now he is out of a job and has plenty of time to be king, for he can sew on his own buttons. What do you say, Cap'n Joe?"

"Oh, I don't mind," agreed Cap'n Joe; "that is, if you all want me to rule you."

"We do!" shouted the slaves, glad to find some one willing to take the job.

"But I'll want a few pointers," continued Cap'n Bill's brother. "I ain't used to this sort o' work, you know, an' if I ain't properly posted I'm liable to make mistakes."

"Sacho will tell you," said Tom Atto, encouragingly. "And now I must go back to the kitchen and look after my dumplings, or you people won't have any dinner to-day."

"Very well," announced Sacho. "I hereby proclaim Cap'n Joe elected King of the Castle—which is the Enchanted Castle no longer. You may all return to your work."

The slaves went away well contented, and the boy and Cap'n Joe now came forward to greet their visitors.

"We're on our way home," explained Cap'n Bill, "an' we don't expec' to travel this way again. But it pleases me to know, Joe, that you're the king o' such a fine castle, an' I'll rest easier now that you're well pervided for."

"Oh, I'm all right, Bill," returned Cap'n Joe. "It's an easy life here, an' a peaceful one. I wish you was as well fixed."

"If ever you need friends, Sacho, or any assistance or counsel, come to me," said the Mermaid Queen to the boy.

"Thank you, madam," he replied. "Now that Zog has

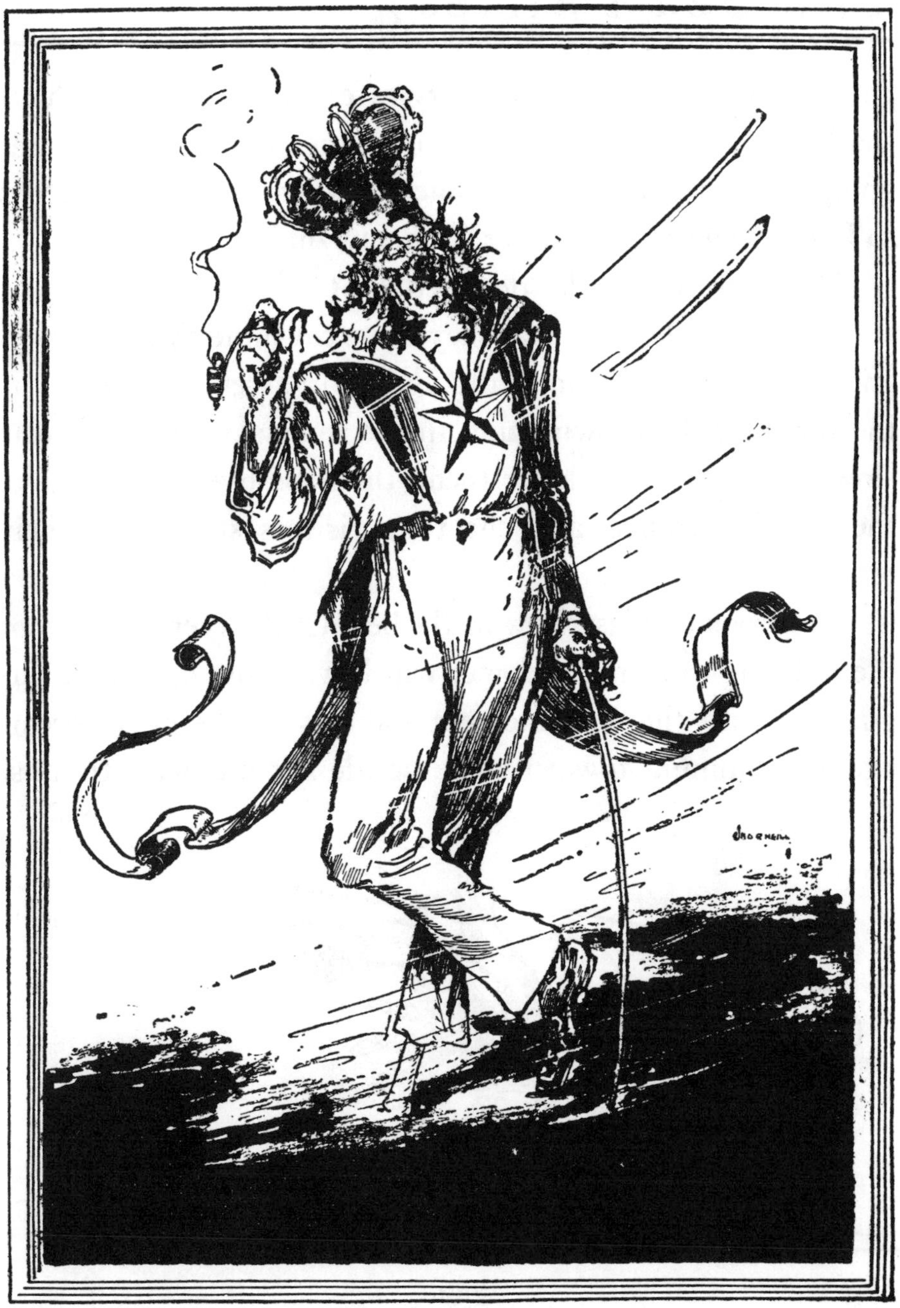

gone, I am sure we shall be very safe and contented. But I shall not forget to come to you if we need you. We are not going to waste any time in anger, or revenge, or evil deeds; so I believe we shall prosper from now on."

"I 'm sure you will," declared Trot.

They now decided that they must continue their journey, and as neither Sacho nor King Joe could ascend to the top of the dome, without swimming in the human way, which was slow and tedious work for them, the good-byes were said at the castle entrance, and the four visitors started on their return.

Trot took one last view of the beautiful silver castle from the hole high up in the dome, which was now open and unguarded, and the next moment she was in the broad ocean again, swimming toward home beside her mermaid friends.

TROT LIVES TO TELL THE TALE

Chap. 22

AQUAREINE was thoughtful for a time. Then she drew
from her finger a ring—a plain gold band, set with a pearl
of great value—and gave it to the little girl.

"If at any period of your life the mermaids can be of ser-
vice to you, my dear," she said, "you have but to come to the
edge of the ocean and call 'Aquareine.' If you are wearing
this ring at the time I shall instantly hear you and come to
your assistance."

"Thank you!" cried the child, slipping the ring over her
own chubby finger, which it fitted perfectly. "I shall never
forget that I have good and loyal friends in the ocean, you
may be sure."

Away and away they swam, swiftly and in a straight line,
keeping in the middle water where they were not liable to
meet many sea people. They passed a few schools of

fishes, where the teachers were explaining to the young ones how to swim properly, and to conduct themselves in a dignified manner; but Trot did not care to stop and watch the exercises.

Although the queen had lost her fairy wand in Zog's domed chamber, she had still enough magic power to carry them all across the ocean in wonderfully quick time, and before Trot and Cap'n Bill were aware of the distance they had come the mermaids paused, while Princess Clia said:

"Now we must go a little deeper, for here is the Giant's Cave, and the entrance to it is near the bottom of the sea."

"What, already!" cried the girl, joyfully; and then through the darker water they swam, passing through the rocky entrance, and began to ascend slowly into the azure-blue water of the cave.

"You've been awfully good to us, and I don't know jus' how to thank you," said Trot, earnestly.

"We have enjoyed your visit to us," said beautiful Queen Aquareine, smiling upon her little friend, "and you may easily repay any pleasure we have given you by speaking well of the mermaids when you hear ignorant earth people condemning us."

"I'll do that, of course," exclaimed the child.

"How 'bout changin' us back to our reg'lar shapes?" inquired Cap'n Bill, anxiously.

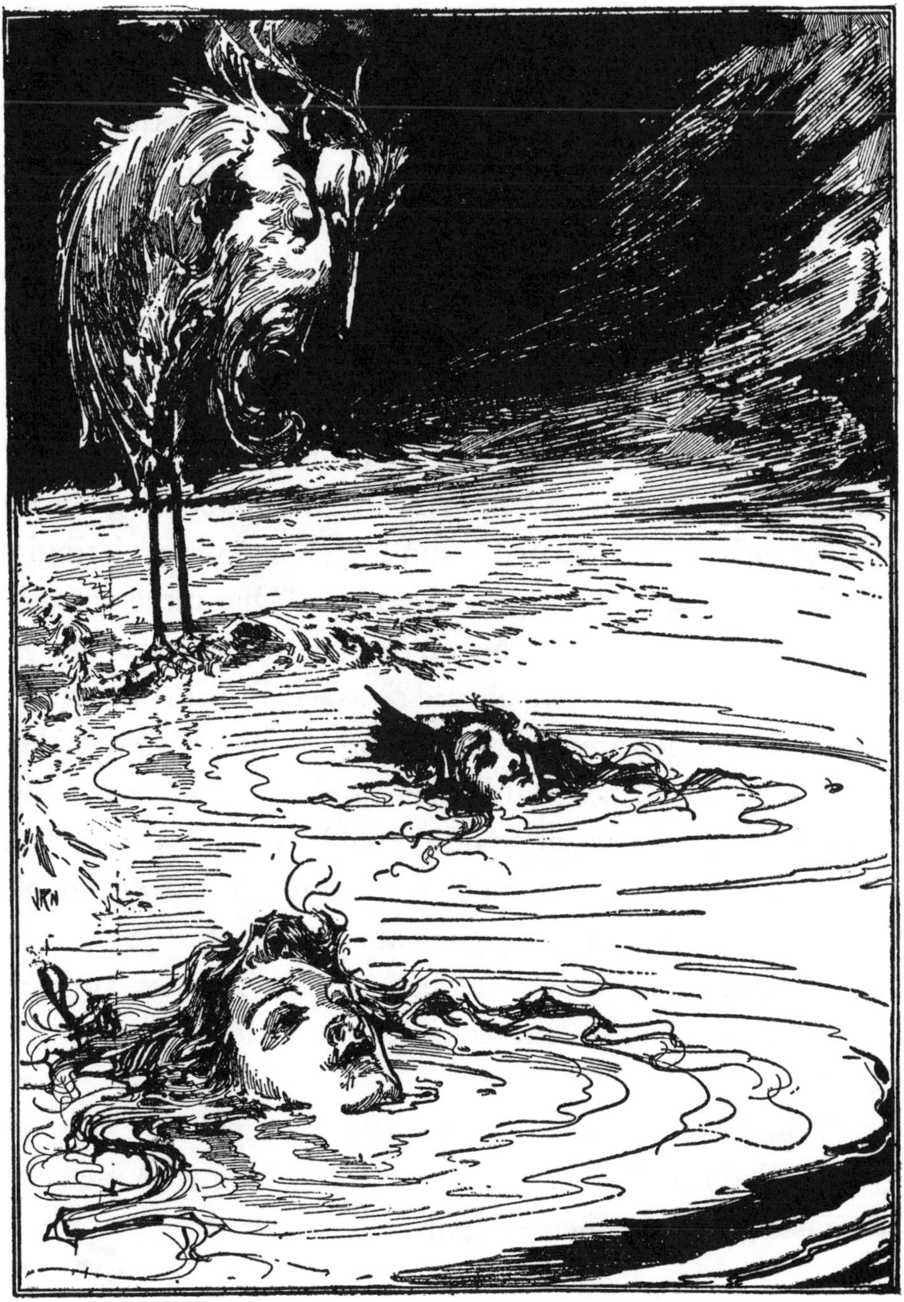

"That will be very easy," replied Princess Clia, with her merry laugh. "See! here we are at the surface of the water."

They pushed their heads above the blue water and looked around the cave. It was silent and deserted. Floating gently near the spot where they had left it was their own little boat.

Cap'n Bill swam to it, took hold of the side, and then turned an inquiring face toward the mermaids.

"Climb in," said the Queen.

So he pulled himself up and awkwardly tumbled forward into the boat. As he did so he heard his wooden leg clatter against the seat, and turned around to look at it wonderingly.

"It's me, all right!" he muttered. "One meat one, an' one hick'ry one. That's the same as belongs to me!"

"Will you lift Mayre aboard?" asked Princess Clia.

The old sailor aroused himself, and as Trot lifted up her arms he seized them and drew her safely into the boat. She was dressed just as usual, and her chubby legs wore shoes and stockings. Strangely enough, neither of them were at all wet, or even damp in any part of their clothing.

"I wonder where our legs have been while we've been gone?" mused Cap'n Bill, gazing at his little friend in great delight.

"And I wonder what's become of our pretty pink and green scaled tails!" returned the girl, laughing with glee, for it seemed good to be herself again.

Chapter Twenty-Two

Queen Aquareine and Princess Clia were a little way off, lying with their pretty faces just out of the water, while their hair floated in soft clouds around them.

"Good-bye, friends!" they called.

"Good-bye!" shouted both Trot and Cap'n Bill, and the little girl blew two kisses from her fingers toward the mermaids.

Then the faces disappeared, leaving little ripples on the surface of the water.

Cap'n Bill picked up the oars and slowly headed the boat toward the mouth of the cave.

"I wonder, Trot, if your ma has missed us," he remarked, uneasily.

"Of course not," replied the girl. "She's been sound asleep, you know."

As the boat crept out into the bright sunlight they were both silent; but each sighed with pleasure at beholding their own everyday world again.

Finally Trot said, softly:

"The land's the best, Cap'n."

"It is, mate; for livin' on," he answered.

"But, I'm glad to have seen the mermaids," she added.

"Well, so'm I, Trot," he agreed. "But, I wouldn't 'a' believed any mortal could ever 'a' seen 'em an'—an'—"

Trot laughed merrily.

"An' lived to tell the tale!" she cried, her eyes dancing with mischief. "Oh, Cap'n Bill, how little we mortals know!"

"True enough, mate," he replied; "but we 're a-learnin' something ev'ry day."

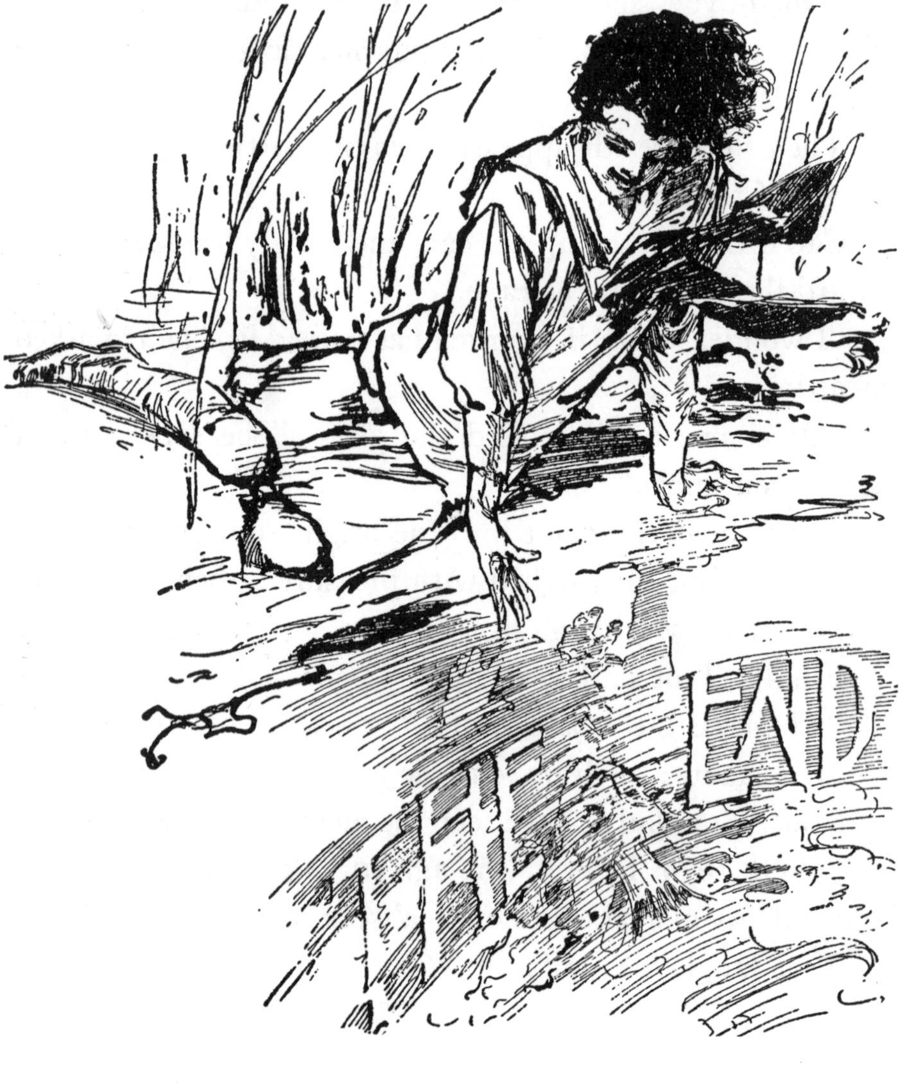
THE END